Housepets! Don't Criticize Your Lovelife

By Rick Griffin

www.housepetscomic.com

Printed by Createspace
A DBA of On-Demand Publishing LLC

Print On Demand Edition

Some other text goes here, perhaps
Copyright © 2014 Rick Griffin

In their heyday, comics were a dominant force in popular culture, but that's over.

–Garry Trudeau

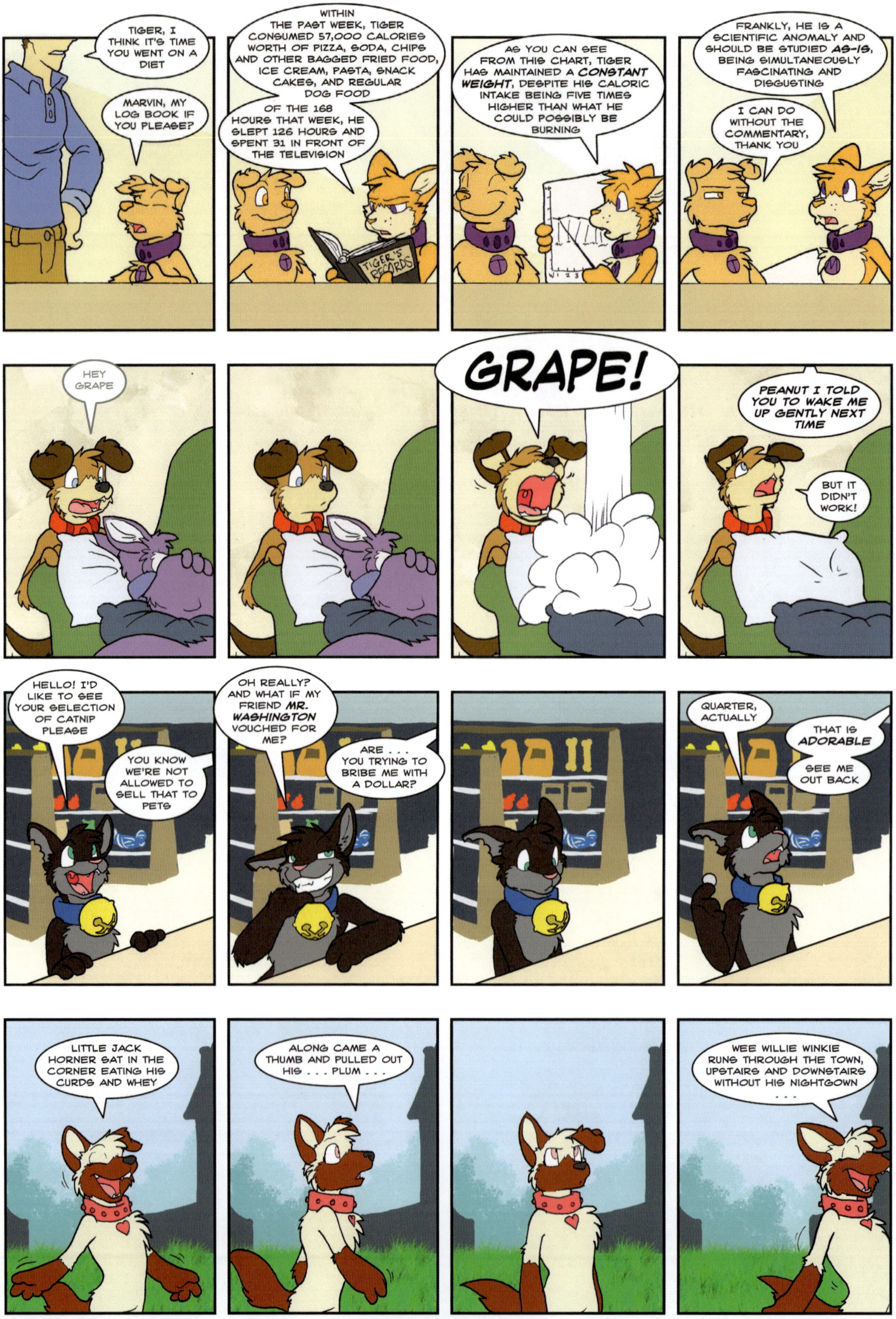
TIGER, I THINK IT'S TIME YOU WENT ON A DIET
MARVIN, MY LOG BOOK IF YOU PLEASE?
WITHIN THE PAST WEEK, TIGER CONSUMED 57,000 CALORIES WORTH OF PIZZA, SODA, CHIPS AND OTHER BAGGED FRIED FOOD, ICE CREAM, PASTA, SNACK CAKES, AND REGULAR DOG FOOD
OF THE 168 HOURS THAT WEEK, HE SLEPT 126 HOURS AND SPENT 31 IN FRONT OF THE TELEVISION
TIGER'S RECORDS
AS YOU CAN SEE FROM THIS CHART, TIGER HAS MAINTAINED A CONSTANT WEIGHT, DESPITE HIS CALORIC INTAKE BEING FIVE TIMES HIGHER THAN WHAT HE COULD POSSIBLY BE BURNING
FRANKLY, HE IS A SCIENTIFIC ANOMALY AND SHOULD BE STUDIED AS-IS, BEING SIMULTANEOUSLY FASCINATING AND DISGUSTING
I CAN DO WITHOUT THE COMMENTARY, THANK YOU
HEY GRAPE
GRAPE!
PEANUT I TOLD YOU TO WAKE ME UP GENTLY NEXT TIME
BUT IT DIDN'T WORK!
HELLO! I'D LIKE TO SEE YOUR SELECTION OF CATNIP PLEASE
YOU KNOW WE'RE NOT ALLOWED TO SELL THAT TO PETS
OH REALLY? AND WHAT IF MY FRIEND MR. WASHINGTON VOUCHED FOR ME?
ARE . . . YOU TRYING TO BRIBE ME WITH A DOLLAR?
QUARTER, ACTUALLY
THAT IS ADORABLE
SEE ME OUT BACK
LITTLE JACK HORNER SAT IN THE CORNER EATING HIS CURDS AND WHEY
ALONG CAME A THUMB AND PULLED OUT HIS . . . PLUM . . .
WEE WILLIE WINKIE RUNS THROUGH THE TOWN, UPSTAIRS AND DOWNSTAIRS WITHOUT HIS NIGHTGOWN . . .

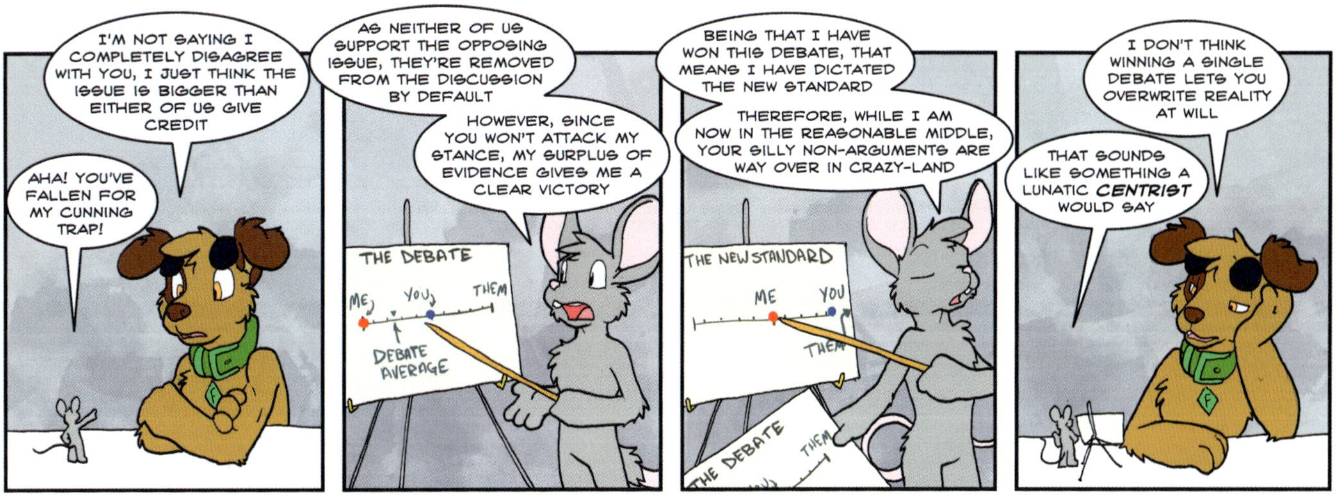

Let's Imaginate: Guys and Dolls!

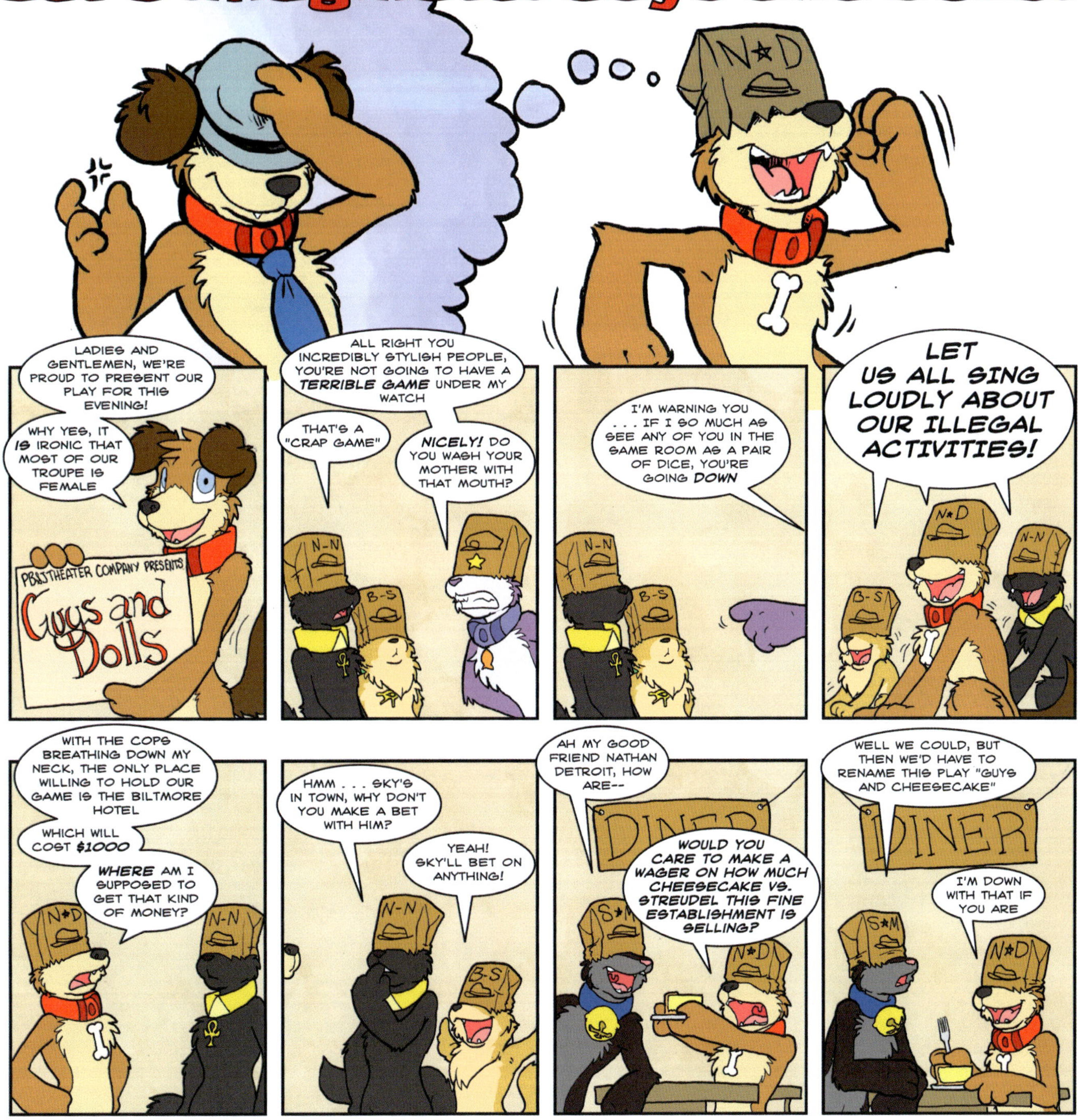

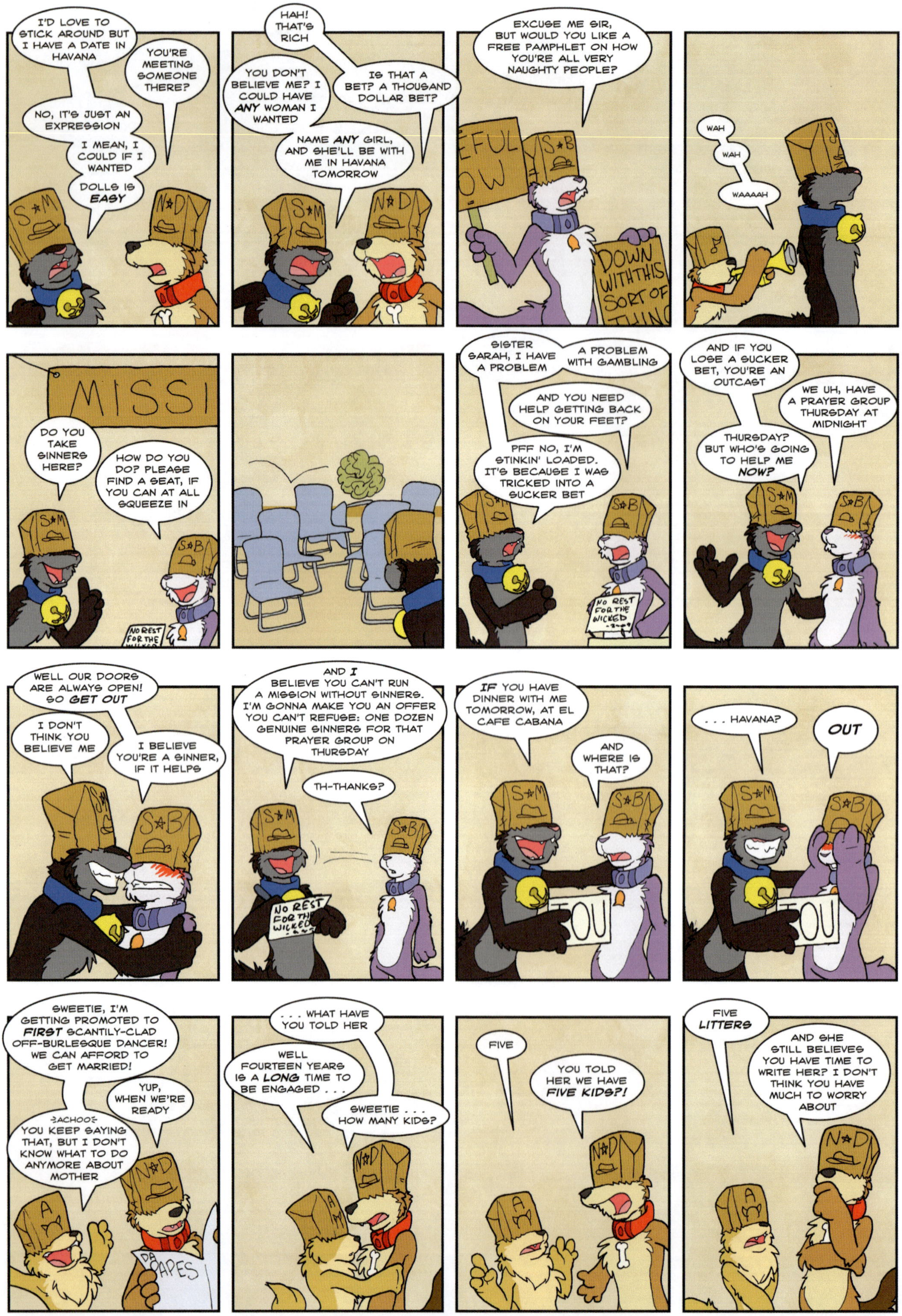
I'D LOVE TO STICK AROUND BUT I HAVE A DATE IN HAVANA
YOU'RE MEETING SOMEONE THERE?
NO, IT'S JUST AN EXPRESSION
I MEAN, I COULD IF I WANTED
DOLLS IS *EASY*
HAH! THAT'S RICH
YOU DON'T BELIEVE ME? I COULD HAVE **ANY** WOMAN I WANTED
IS THAT A BET? A THOUSAND DOLLAR BET?
NAME **ANY** GIRL, AND SHE'LL BE WITH ME IN HAVANA TOMORROW
EXCUSE ME SIR, BUT WOULD YOU LIKE A FREE PAMPHLET ON HOW YOU'RE ALL VERY NAUGHTY PEOPLE?
DOWN WITH THIS SORT OF
WAH
WAH
WAAAAH
MISSI
DO YOU TAKE SINNERS HERE?
HOW DO YOU DO? PLEASE FIND A SEAT, IF YOU CAN AT ALL SQUEEZE IN
NO REST FOR THE
SISTER SARAH, I HAVE A PROBLEM
A PROBLEM WITH GAMBLING
AND YOU NEED HELP GETTING BACK ON YOUR FEET?
PFF NO, I'M STINKIN' LOADED. IT'S BECAUSE I WAS TRICKED INTO A SUCKER BET
NO REST FOR THE WICKED
AND IF YOU LOSE A SUCKER BET, YOU'RE AN OUTCAST
WE UH, HAVE A PRAYER GROUP THURSDAY AT MIDNIGHT
THURSDAY? BUT WHO'S GOING TO HELP ME *NOW?*
WELL OUR DOORS ARE ALWAYS OPEN! SO *GET OUT*
I DON'T THINK YOU BELIEVE ME
I BELIEVE YOU'RE A SINNER, IF IT HELPS
AND *I* BELIEVE YOU CAN'T RUN A MISSION WITHOUT SINNERS. I'M GONNA MAKE YOU AN OFFER YOU CAN'T REFUSE: ONE DOZEN GENUINE SINNERS FOR THAT PRAYER GROUP ON THURSDAY
TH-THANKS?
NO REST FOR THE WICKED
IF YOU HAVE DINNER WITH ME TOMORROW, AT EL CAFE CABANA
AND WHERE IS THAT?
IOU
. . . HAVANA?
OUT
IOU
SWEETIE, I'M GETTING PROMOTED TO ***FIRST*** SCANTILY-CLAD OFF-BURLESQUE DANCER! WE CAN AFFORD TO GET MARRIED!
YUP, WHEN WE'RE READY
ACHOO
YOU KEEP SAYING THAT, BUT I DON'T KNOW WHAT TO DO ANYMORE ABOUT MOTHER
DA PAPES
. . . WHAT HAVE YOU TOLD HER
WELL FOURTEEN YEARS IS A ***LONG*** TIME TO BE ENGAGED . . .
SWEETIE . . . HOW MANY KIDS?
FIVE
YOU TOLD HER WE HAVE ***FIVE KIDS?!***
FIVE ***LITTERS***
AND SHE STILL BELIEVES YOU HAVE TIME TO WRITE HER? I DON'T THINK YOU HAVE MUCH TO WORRY ABOUT

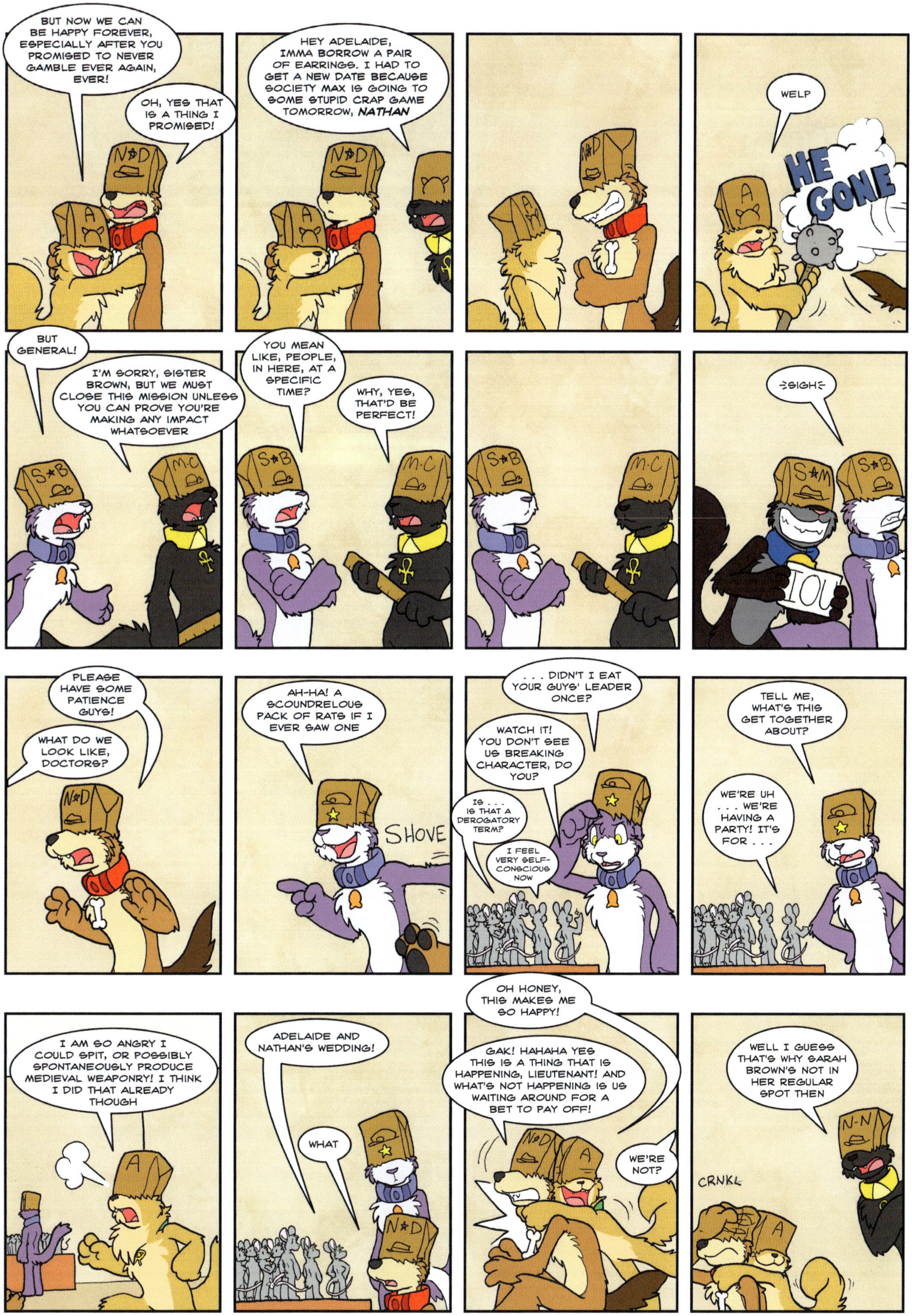
BUT NOW WE CAN BE HAPPY FOREVER, ESPECIALLY AFTER YOU PROMISED TO NEVER GAMBLE EVER AGAIN, EVER!
OH, YES THAT IS A THING I PROMISED!
HEY ADELAIDE, IMMA BORROW A PAIR OF EARRINGS. I HAD TO GET A NEW DATE BECAUSE SOCIETY MAX IS GOING TO SOME STUPID CRAP GAME TOMORROW, NATHAN
WELP
HE GONE
BUT GENERAL!
I'M SORRY, SISTER BROWN, BUT WE MUST CLOSE THIS MISSION UNLESS YOU CAN PROVE YOU'RE MAKING ANY IMPACT WHATSOEVER
YOU MEAN LIKE, PEOPLE, IN HERE, AT A SPECIFIC TIME?
WHY, YES, THAT'D BE PERFECT!
=SIGH=
IOU
PLEASE HAVE SOME PATIENCE GUYS!
WHAT DO WE LOOK LIKE, DOCTORS?
AH-HA! A SCOUNDRELOUS PACK OF RATS IF I EVER SAW ONE
SHOVE
. . . DIDN'T I EAT YOUR GUYS' LEADER ONCE?
WATCH IT! YOU DON'T SEE US BREAKING CHARACTER, DO YOU?
IS . . . IS THAT A DEROGATORY TERM?
I FEEL VERY SELF-CONSCIOUS NOW
TELL ME, WHAT'S THIS GET TOGETHER ABOUT?
WE'RE UH . . . WE'RE HAVING A PARTY! IT'S FOR . . .
I AM SO ANGRY I COULD SPIT, OR POSSIBLY SPONTANEOUSLY PRODUCE MEDIEVAL WEAPONRY! I THINK I DID THAT ALREADY THOUGH
ADELAIDE AND NATHAN'S WEDDING!
WHAT
OH HONEY, THIS MAKES ME SO HAPPY!
GAK! HAHAHA YES THIS IS A THING THAT IS HAPPENING, LIEUTENANT! AND WHAT'S NOT HAPPENING IS US WAITING AROUND FOR A BET TO PAY OFF!
WE'RE NOT?
WELL I GUESS THAT'S WHY SARAH BROWN'S NOT IN HER REGULAR SPOT THEN
CRNKL

THIS *DULCE DE LECHE* IS DELICIOUS! AND YOU'RE SURE IT ISN'T ALCOHOLIC?
OH WELL YOU KNOW . . . A LITTLE, AS A PRESERVATIVE
YOU SAID THE SAME THING ABOUT THE LONG ISLAND ICE TEA
AND THE ROOT BEER SHOOTERS
AND THE IRISH CAR BOMB
IT'S HOT IN CUBA, AND THEY NEED TO . . . PRESERVE . . .
YOU KNOW WHAT, YOU'RE RIGHT. I HAVEN'T BEEN ENTIRELY HONEST WITH YOU
¡MESERO! UN *ORANGE SODA* PARA LA SEÑORA, POR FAVOR
AND YOU SPEAK SPANISH! THIS IS SO *AWESOME!*
LATER BACK IN NEW YORK
(BECAUSE APPARENTLY SKY HAD NO REAL REASON TO BE IN CUBA)
I HAD A GREAT TIME, SKY
AND YOU ONLY THREW UP FOUR TIMES! IT WENT PRETTY GOOD
EVEN THOUGH I DON'T REMEMBER MUCH OF WHAT HAPPENED, SKY . . . I THINK I LO--
IT DA PO-PO! EVERYONE SCAT!
MISSION
OH RIGHT, WE'RE APPROACHING THE PLAY'S SECOND REVERSAL OF FORTUNE SO *I HATE YOU NOW AND BLAME THIS ON YOU!*
I'LL GO GET READY FOR THE ENDING
HOW'S IT GOING, NICELY?
NICELY
DOESN'T LOOK LIKE IT
IT'S THE NAME OF THIS VODKA
NICELY, WERE YOU GUYS SHOOTING DICE IN THE MISSION LAST NIGHT?
YEAH, BUT WE BROKE WHEN BIG JULE WAS STILL OUT 10K, AND HE ASKED THE GAME CONTINUE
WITH A GUN
SO WHY ARE YOU *HERE*?
EASY! IF YOU TAKE ME TO WHEREVER NATE IS NOW, *I'LL* TALK TO ADELAIDE
NATE TOLD ME TO EXPLAIN THINGS TO ADELAIDE . . . SKY I CAN'T DO IT!
HOW DO YOU PLAN ON DOING THAT?
HEY ADELAIDE, WHAT DO YOU THINK OF NATE?
HE'S A MEAN OL' JERK FOR STANDING ME UP TO GO GAMBLING!
SO HOW COME YOU FELL IN LOVE WITH A GAMBLER?
'CAUSE HE'S SUAVE AND COOL AND DANGEROUS AND I LOVE HIM AGAIN
SOON!
ALRIGHT YALL'S MUGS, BIG NATE IS NOW OUT 25K AND NOT NOBODY IS LEAVING TIL HE GETS HIM--
STAMP
OH HEY GUYS. SO, I HAVE A DEBT I NEED TO SETTLE, AND I NEED YOU ALL TO ATTEND A PRAYER MEETING IN ABOUT THIRTY MINUTES
WHAT?!
BOO!
HOW ABOUT FOR A CHANCE TO WIN SOME MONEY?
THAT WOULD HAVE ALARMING MORAL IMPLICATIONS!
I'M NOT ASKING FOR YOUR MORALS, JUST YOUR BUTTS IN SEATS FOR ABOUT AN HOUR
THEN *YES*
MY BUTT IS *ALWAYS* FOR SALE!

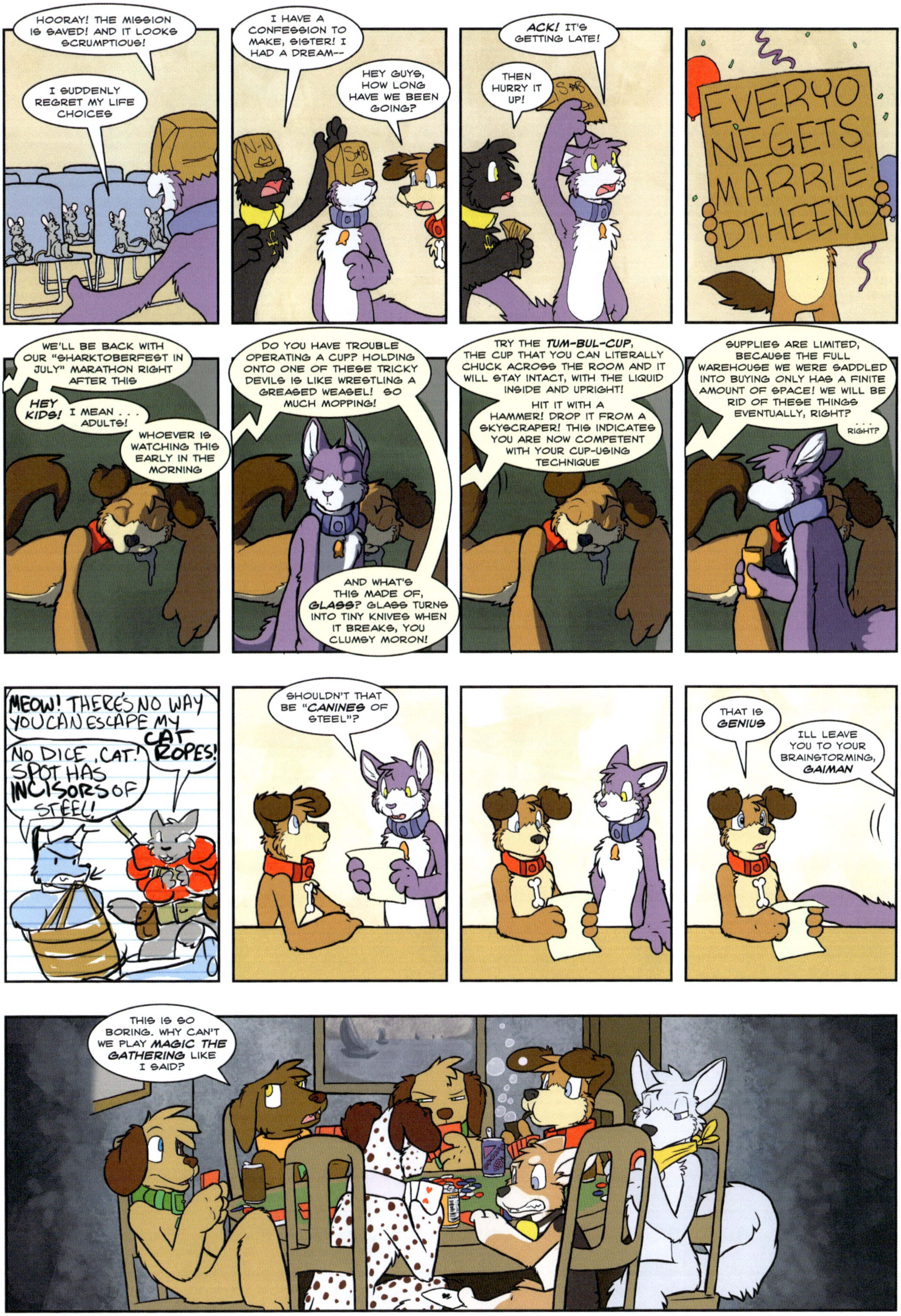
HOORAY! THE MISSION IS SAVED! AND IT LOOKS SCRUMPTIOUS!
I SUDDENLY REGRET MY LIFE CHOICES
I HAVE A CONFESSION TO MAKE, SISTER! I HAD A DREAM--
HEY GUYS, HOW LONG HAVE WE BEEN GOING?
ACK! IT'S GETTING LATE!
THEN HURRY IT UP!
EVERYONEGETS MARRIEDTHEEND
WE'LL BE BACK WITH OUR "SHARKTOBERFEST IN JULY" MARATHON RIGHT AFTER THIS
HEY KIDS! I MEAN . . . ADULTS!
WHOEVER IS WATCHING THIS EARLY IN THE MORNING
DO YOU HAVE TROUBLE OPERATING A CUP? HOLDING ONTO ONE OF THESE TRICKY DEVILS IS LIKE WRESTLING A GREASED WEASEL! SO MUCH MOPPING!
AND WHAT'S THIS MADE OF, GLASS? GLASS TURNS INTO TINY KNIVES WHEN IT BREAKS, YOU CLUMSY MORON!
TRY THE TUM-BUL-CUP, THE CUP THAT YOU CAN LITERALLY CHUCK ACROSS THE ROOM AND IT WILL STAY INTACT, WITH THE LIQUID INSIDE AND UPRIGHT!
HIT IT WITH A HAMMER! DROP IT FROM A SKYSCRAPER! THIS INDICATES YOU ARE NOW COMPETENT WITH YOUR CUP-USING TECHNIQUE
SUPPLIES ARE LIMITED, BECAUSE THE FULL WAREHOUSE WE WERE SADDLED INTO BUYING ONLY HAS A FINITE AMOUNT OF SPACE! WE WILL BE RID OF THESE THINGS EVENTUALLY, RIGHT?
. . . RIGHT?
MEOW! THERE'S NO WAY YOU CAN ESCAPE MY CAT ROPES!
NO DICE, CAT! SPOT HAS INCISORS OF STEEL!
SHOULDN'T THAT BE "CANINES OF STEEL"?
THAT IS GENIUS
ILL LEAVE YOU TO YOUR BRAINSTORMING, GAIMAN
THIS IS SO BORING. WHY CAN'T WE PLAY MAGIC THE GATHERING LIKE I SAID?

SANDWICH-HANCHO, I MUST APOLOGIZE DEEPLY! SUMMER EXAMS ARE APPROACHING AND I NEED SOME EXTRA--
THAT'S FINE WITH ME
--TIME OFF TO . . . NANI? JUST LIKE THAT? I'VE BEEN PRACTICING IN FRONT OF THE MIRROR AND EVERYTHING!
DON'T TAKE THIS THE WRONG WAY, BUT I NOTICED YOU SNEAKING STUDY INTO YOUR BREAK TIME, SO I WAS EXPECTING THIS
MOUSHIWAKE ARIMASEN! I DID NOT MEAN TO TAKE UP VALUABLE COMPANY TIME--
NO, THAT'S A GOOD THING! SCHOOL IS IMPORTANT, SO LONG AS YOU GET YOUR WORK DONE
LOOK, ARE YOU GOING TO LET ME FINISH, BECAUSE I'M NOT WASTING A PERFECTLY GOOD APOLOGY
I'M SORRY. YOUR GROVELING IS CUTE, THOUGH
YOU'LL HAVE TWO HOURS TO COMPLETE THE TEST. BE SURE TO TURN IT IN FACE-DOWN ON THE TABLE AND GRAB A COURSE EVALUATION PACKET RIGHT AFTER
SONO SHIROI KURIIMU NO SHITA DE YAWARAKAI SUPONJI WO KASANETE
YASASHISA MO ITOSHISA MO NOSETE PAN! PAN! AMAI AMAI PAPA NO PANKEEKI GA
PAN! PAN! TSUTSUMIKONDERU NO--BEEP
YOU HAVE CANCELLED YOUR CALL, IT WILL BE SENT TO YOUR VOICEMAIL! BEEP
ARE YOU SURE YOU WANT TO ENTER SILENT MODE? THIS MODE IS USEFUL IF YOU WISH TO ENTER A QUIET AREA, SUCH AS A THEATER OR A FANCY RESTAURANT BEEP
YOUR PHONE IS NOW SHUTTING DOWN
BEE-DEEP EE-DOOP BOOP BWAA
BOW BOW BEE DOOP EE DOOP BOO
I AM DEEPLY REGRETFUL OF MY CONDUCT DURING THE TEST, SENSEI. I BEG YOU, DO NOT FAIL ME FOR BREAKING CLASSROOM RULES
DON'T BE SILLY. MY PHONE GOES OFF ALL THE TIME
HOWEVER, PERHAPS TO THE RELIEF OF THE OTHER STUDENTS, YOU DID NOT BREAK THE CURVE THIS TIME
SLEEP IS MORE IMPORTANT THAN LAST-MINUTE STUDY, AND I HOPE YOU'LL REMEMBER THAT NEXT SEMESTER
67?! WHAT AM I SUPPOSED TO TELL MY FATHER?! HOW AM I SUPPOSED TO JUSTIFY MY STUDENT VISA WITH SUCH A POOR GRADE?
YOU STILL HAVE AN A AVERAGE, MR. KITAMURA. YOUR GPA IS UNAFFECTED
DOESN'T ANYONE KNOW HOW TO ALLOCATE SHAME IN THIS COUNTRY?

Testing Grounds

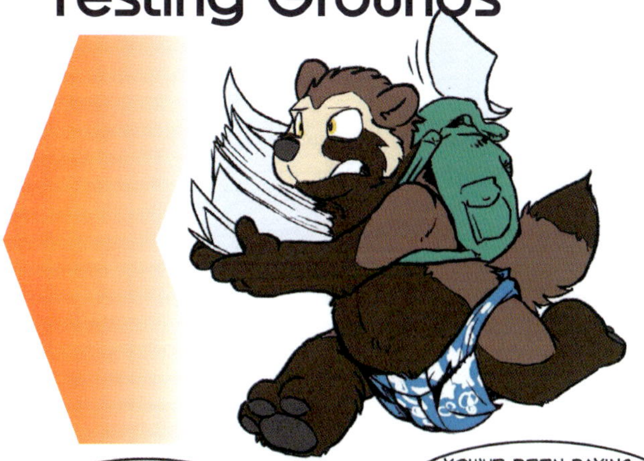

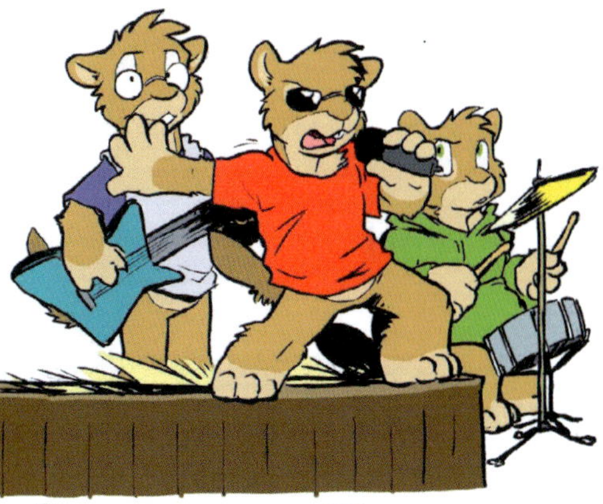

Taking Cover

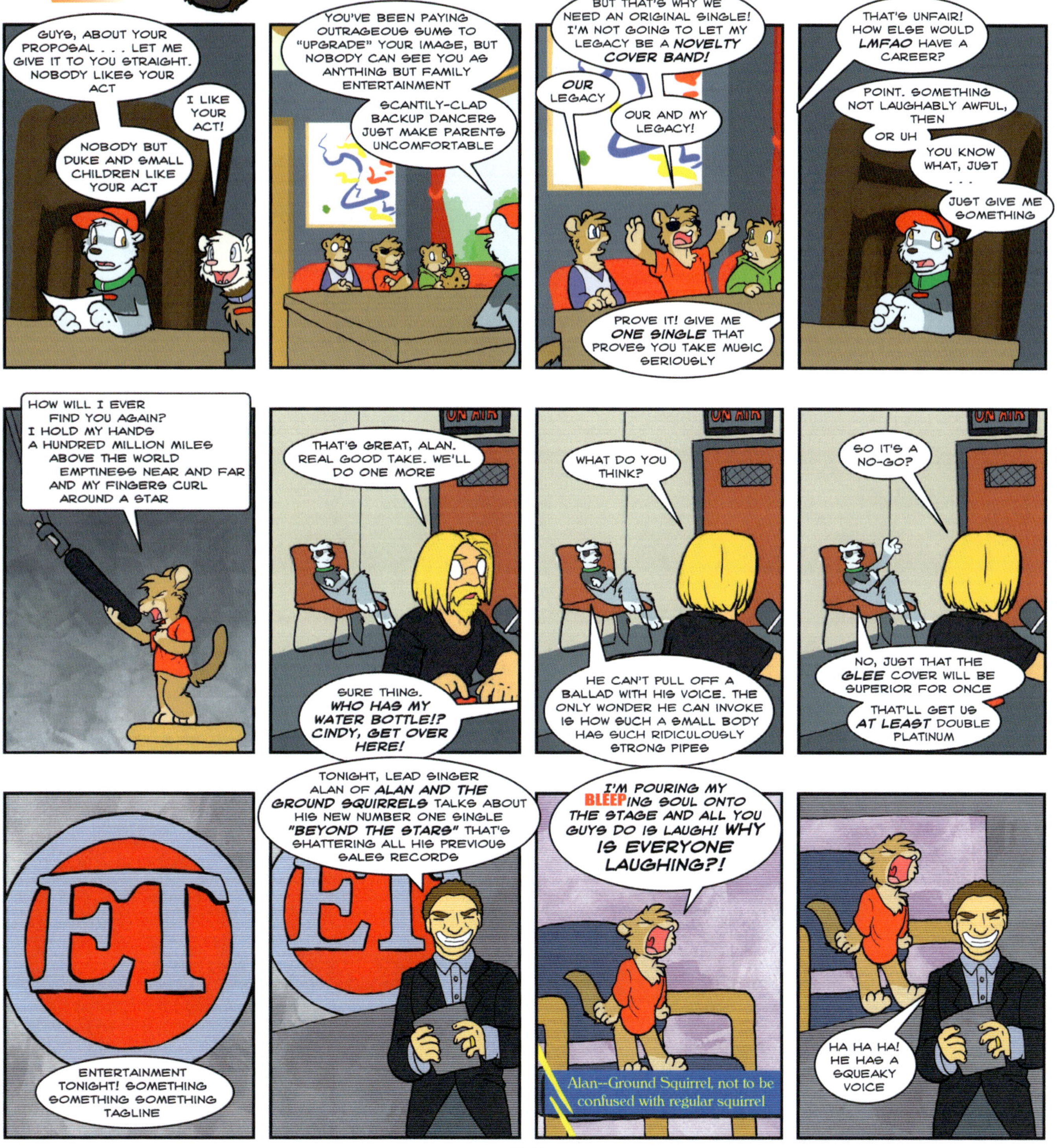

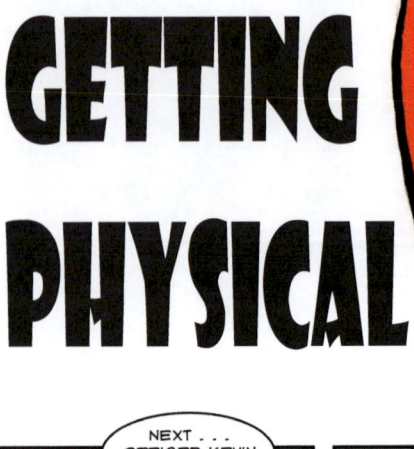

GETTING PHYSICAL

Panel 1: "NEXT... OFFICER KEVIN BEAUREGARD" / "HERE!"

Panel 2: "SIR! I HEREBY OFFER AS MY SOLEMN PLEDGE THAT I WILL PERFORM THIS PHYSICAL TO THE BEST OF MY ABILITY AND MAKE MY SQUAD AND MY COUNTRY PROUD!"

Panel 3: "MY BLOOD WORK, AS REQUESTED, DONE LAST WEEK SO THE BLOOD LOSS WOULD NOT INHIBIT MY PERFORMANCE!"

Panel 4: "GO TEAM USA WOOOO" / "YOU'LL HAVE TO FORGIVE HIM; HE GETS A LITTLE PUMPED UP THE WEEK AFTER THE OLYMPICS"

Panel 5: "THAT'S ENOUGH, KEVIN. LET'S TALK FOR A SECOND"

Panel 6: "I APPRECIATE YOUR ENTHUSIASM, BUT THE PURPOSE OF A PHYSICAL IS NOT TO SET RECORDS. YOU DON'T NEED TO PERFORM AT A '10'" / PANT PANT

Panel 7: "FOR EXAMPLE, DURING REFLEX TESTS, YOU DON'T NEED TO BEAT YOUR NATURAL REACTION TIME" / PANT PANT

Panel 8: "ALSO, YOU DIDN'T NEED TO FILL THE URINALYSIS JAR TO THE TOP" / "JUST TRYING TO BE ALL I CAN BE SIR!"

Panel 9: "AND FINALLY, YOUR BODY FAT PERCENTAGE IS AT POINT FIVE PERCENT"

Panel 10: "YES! I WIN!" / "THAT'S BAD"

Panel 11: "MINIMUM BODY FAT SHOULD BE THREE PERCENT, ANY LESS IS DETRIMENTAL TO YOUR HEALTH. YOU'LL NEED A CHANGE OF DIET FOR A FEW WEEKS"

Panel 12: "THIS FEELS WRONG" / "MY CONDOLENCES" / *WHOLE MILK* / *DONUT UNTO OTHERS*

PsyCon + PsyCon 2: Psyconner

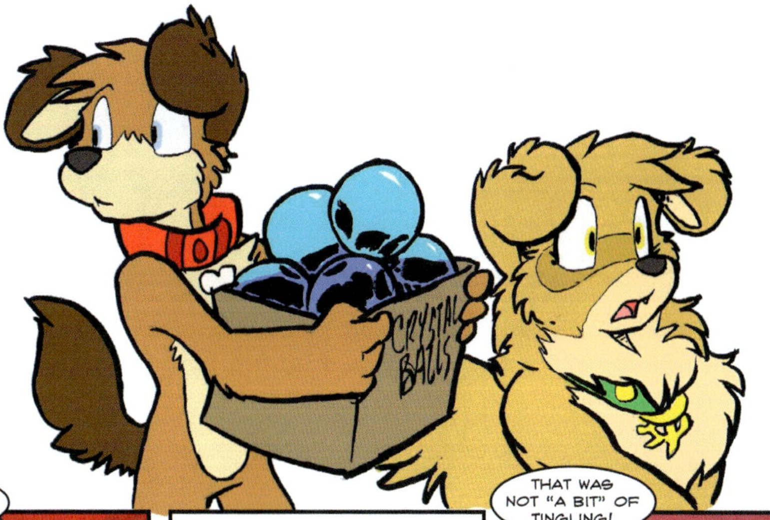

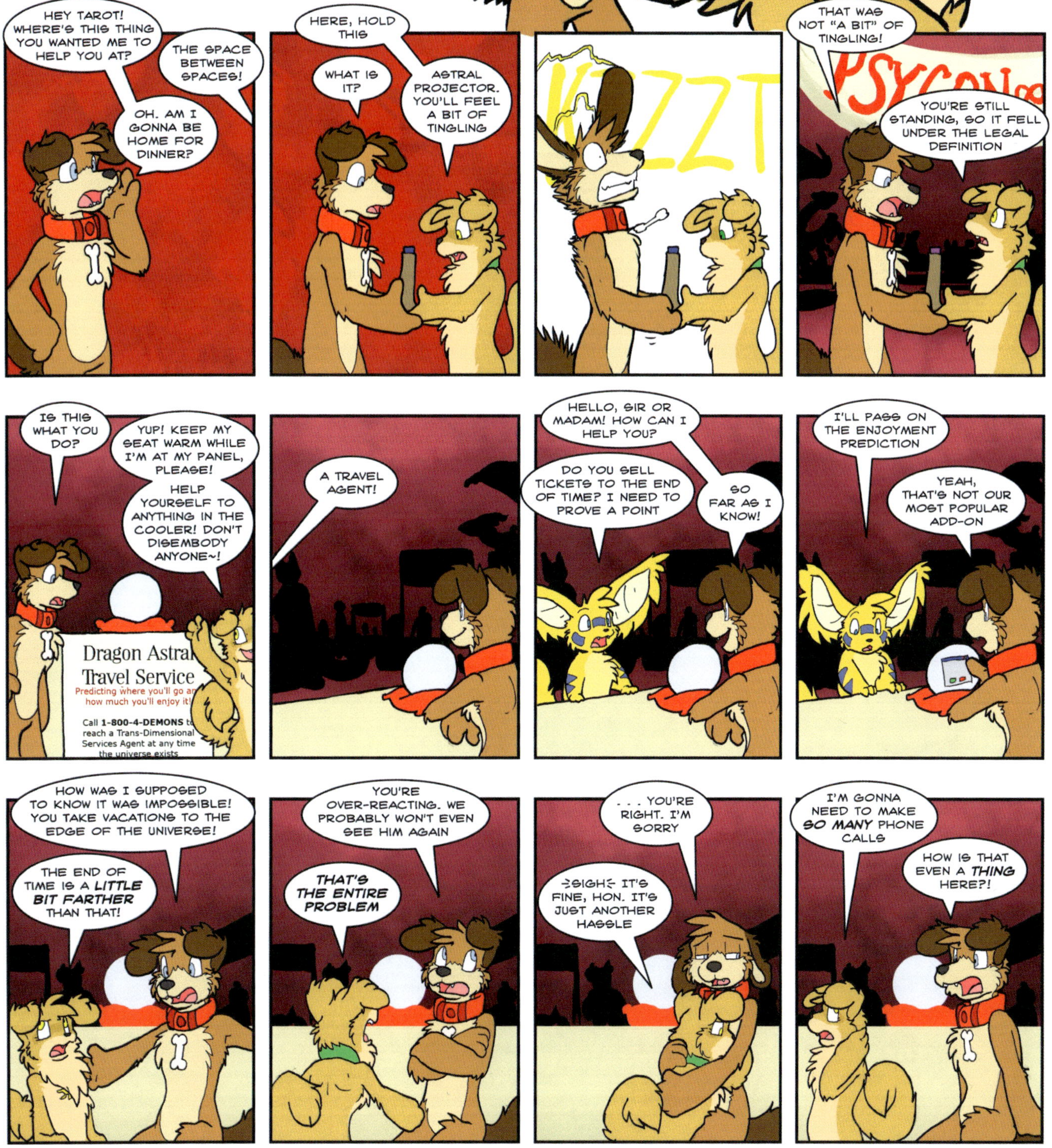

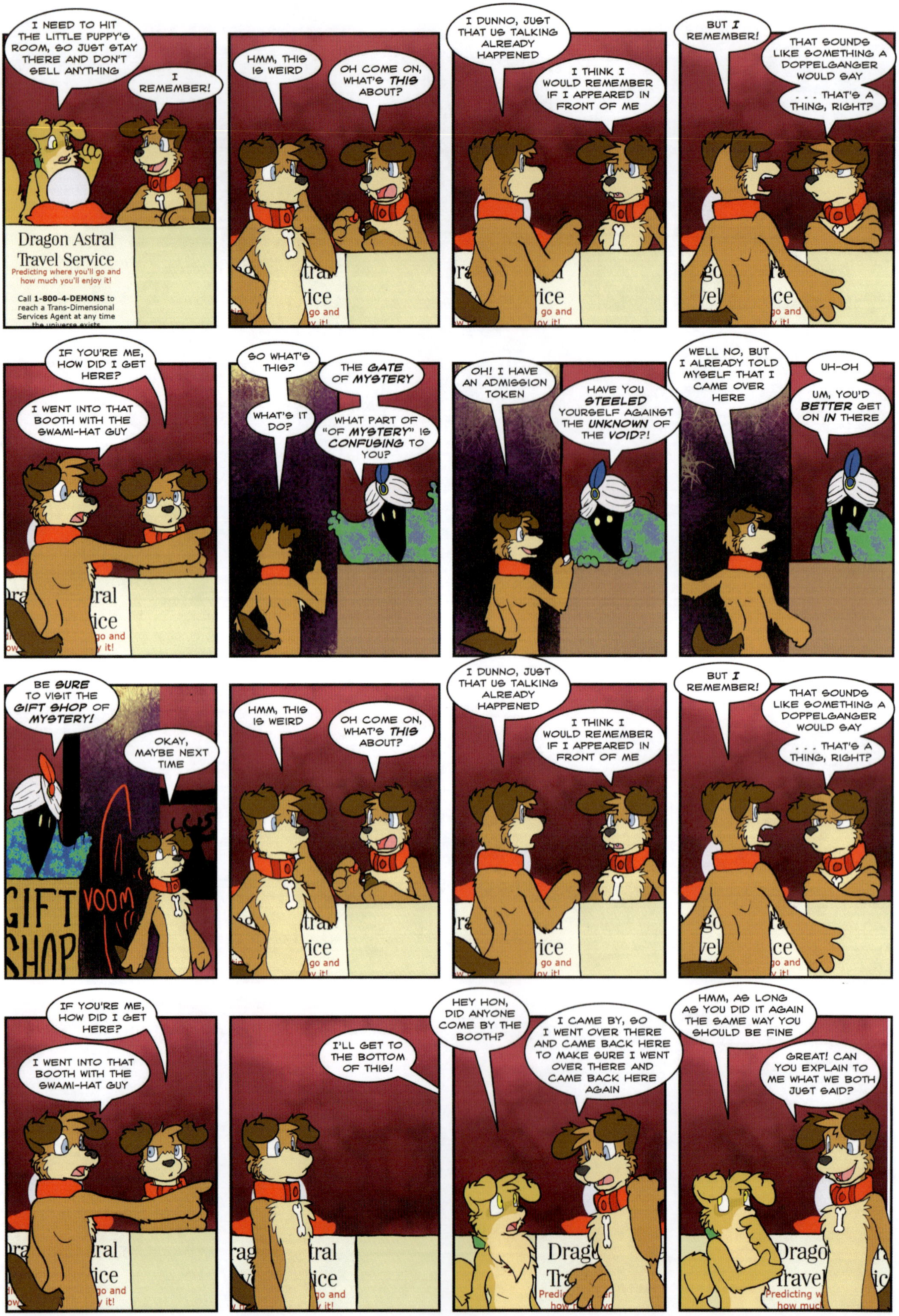
I NEED TO HIT THE LITTLE PUPPY'S ROOM, SO JUST STAY THERE AND DON'T SELL ANYTHING
I REMEMBER!
Dragon Astral Travel Service
Predicting where you'll go and how much you'll enjoy it!
Call 1-800-4-DEMONS to reach a Trans-Dimensional Services Agent at any time
HMM, THIS IS WEIRD
OH COME ON, WHAT'S THIS ABOUT?
I DUNNO, JUST THAT US TALKING ALREADY HAPPENED
I THINK I WOULD REMEMBER IF I APPEARED IN FRONT OF ME
BUT I REMEMBER!
THAT SOUNDS LIKE SOMETHING A DOPPELGANGER WOULD SAY
. . . THAT'S A THING, RIGHT?
IF YOU'RE ME, HOW DID I GET HERE?
I WENT INTO THAT BOOTH WITH THE SWAMI-HAT GUY
SO WHAT'S THIS?
THE GATE OF MYSTERY
WHAT'S IT DO?
WHAT PART OF "OF MYSTERY" IS CONFUSING TO YOU?
OH! I HAVE AN ADMISSION TOKEN
HAVE YOU STEELED YOURSELF AGAINST THE UNKNOWN OF THE VOID?!
WELL NO, BUT I ALREADY TOLD MYSELF THAT I CAME OVER HERE
UH-OH
UM, YOU'D BETTER GET ON IN THERE
BE SURE TO VISIT THE GIFT SHOP OF MYSTERY!
OKAY, MAYBE NEXT TIME
GIFT SHOP
VOOM
HMM, THIS IS WEIRD
OH COME ON, WHAT'S THIS ABOUT?
I DUNNO, JUST THAT US TALKING ALREADY HAPPENED
I THINK I WOULD REMEMBER IF I APPEARED IN FRONT OF ME
BUT I REMEMBER!
THAT SOUNDS LIKE SOMETHING A DOPPELGANGER WOULD SAY
. . . THAT'S A THING, RIGHT?
IF YOU'RE ME, HOW DID I GET HERE?
I WENT INTO THAT BOOTH WITH THE SWAMI-HAT GUY
I'LL GET TO THE BOTTOM OF THIS!
HEY HON, DID ANYONE COME BY THE BOOTH?
I CAME BY, SO I WENT OVER THERE AND CAME BACK HERE TO MAKE SURE I WENT OVER THERE AND CAME BACK HERE AGAIN
HMM, AS LONG AS YOU DID IT AGAIN THE SAME WAY YOU SHOULD BE FINE
GREAT! CAN YOU EXPLAIN TO ME WHAT WE BOTH JUST SAID?

The Retroactively Continuous Adventures of SPOT

Panel 1:
- "Hey Peanut, whatever happened to that story with the cyborg?"
- "What do you mean? He made a bunch of kids fat"

Panel 2:
- "No, I mean the one where you introduced him. Spot and Stripe were tied up and you never finished it"
- "Oh that! That was over here in issue..."

Panel 3:
- "...uh-oh"

Panel 4:
THE ADVENTURES of SPOT (superdog)
SPECIAL **RETCON** ISSUE!

Panel 5:
"I, SPOT (superdog) have apparently lost my memory... but I can't remember what it was or how I lost it!"

Panel 6:
"The only clue I have is this photograph"
"NEVER FORGET! (I totally beat up a robot)"
"Who even took this picture"

Panel 7:
"Hmm, I could figure out this building's location by matching the skyline in the window..."

Panel 8:
"Or I could just look on the back"
"TAKEN 4/14 123 A BUILDING Artwould rescue again"

15

SPOT approaches a bulding
Come, spot (superdog) I have been waiting
What is this place?
A construct of your mind
I anticipated you would return here one day
You! I already defeated you, like, maybe twice!
And you shall continue to defeat me, but to no avail
For you see, nothing you have done for years has ever mattered. These victories you reveled in...
ROBO-EYE
it Has all been a lie
SUPER VR HELM
VR HELM JR.
(Dramatic pan-out)
COME ON! IT CAN BE THE START OF AN AWESOME GRITTY REBOOT!
YOU COULD HAVE DONE THAT WITHOUT INVALIDATING THE CURRENT UNIVERSE!
IT'S NOT INVALIDATED! IT WAS REAL IN A SENSE!
YOU KNOW THAT DOESN'T COUNT!
Unbeknowest to the AI guiding Spot's dream, the ORPHAN-STARS had aligned
From the primordial electric-gamma radiation, the STAR CLONE DREAM BABIES of Spot (superdog) and Stripe were born!
And THEY had all those adventures, mind-linked with the dreaming SPOT all the while!
Still happened!
Arriving in the bulding at the same time as sleeping Spot, STAR CLONE DREAM Spot delivered furious justice to the Cyborg!
Noooo
Upon waking, STAR CLONE DREAM SPOT vanished
What am I doing back here?
Poof
SUPER VR HELM
Would it be forever? ...?
OR YOU COULD HAVE JUST IGNORED THE STORY ALTOGETHER
I DON'T THINK SO; I ALREADY USED THE HISTORY-ERASING PLOT

TEMPLE CRASHERS

Panel 1: "I'm beginning to think going all *BEAU GESTE* was a bad idea"
"YES I know that's North Africa and not Arabia, shut up"

Panel 2: "Alright fine. I'll tell you, but this doesn't increase your share. We're looking for an ancient temple in these hills. Squarish with a dome on top and a rolling slab style door. Now if you have any leads--"

Panel 3: "...What do you MEAN 'like the one Henry Milton imported'?"

Panel 4: "Now, I mighta grew up in the deep woods, quite literally under a rock"
"But shoot, even I know 'bout that temple. Silly to even ask"

Panel 5: "May I remind suh he is not required to make business calls personally"
"I'd rather not too many people know what I'm trying to do, Jeeves. That INCLUDES Mr. Steward"

Panel 6: "I was under the impression that Mr. Steward was chief organizer of the excavation"
"Under protest"

Panel 7: "He's been acting suspicious. I'm only keeping him onboard so I can keep track of him"
"And what is it suh would not like to come to Steward's attention?"

Panel 8: "I'm putting together a raiding party for that temple. It's literally bigger on the inside, hence it's full of mystic(k)al energies, hence we need a psychic, hence the phone call"
"Certainly, suh"

Panel 9: "Then I mentioned to her the temple had dragon and gryphon sigils on it. She screamed and hung up"
"I understand. Has suh tried someone local?"
"I was just about to"

Panel 10: (silent)

Panel 11: "Is suh going to--"
RING :BEEP:

Panel 12: "The best psychics aren't in the phone book"
"Excellent point, suh"
"Tarot's psychic hotline, how will I have helped you?"

17

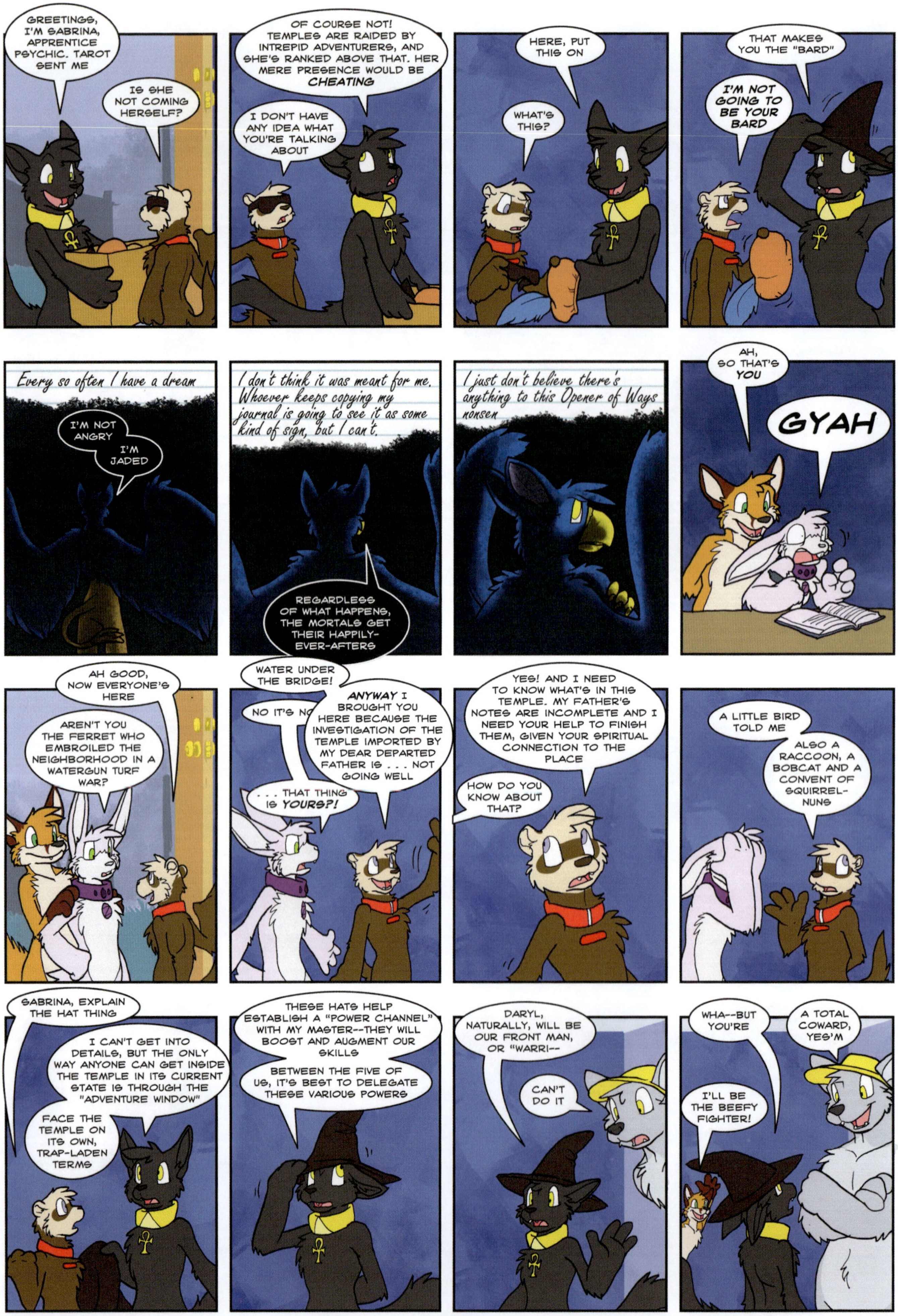
GREETINGS, I'M SABRINA, APPRENTICE PSYCHIC. TAROT SENT ME
IS SHE NOT COMING HERSELF?
OF COURSE NOT! TEMPLES ARE RAIDED BY INTREPID ADVENTURERS, AND SHE'S RANKED ABOVE THAT. HER MERE PRESENCE WOULD BE CHEATING
I DON'T HAVE ANY IDEA WHAT YOU'RE TALKING ABOUT
HERE, PUT THIS ON
WHAT'S THIS?
THAT MAKES YOU THE "BARD"
I'M NOT GOING TO BE YOUR BARD
Every so often I have a dream
I'M NOT ANGRY
I'M JADED
I don't think it was meant for me. Whoever keeps copying my journal is going to see it as some kind of sign, but I can't.
REGARDLESS OF WHAT HAPPENS, THE MORTALS GET THEIR HAPPILY-EVER-AFTERS
I just don't believe there's anything to this Opener of Ways nonsen
AH, SO THAT'S YOU
GYAH
AH GOOD, NOW EVERYONE'S HERE
AREN'T YOU THE FERRET WHO EMBROILED THE NEIGHBORHOOD IN A WATERGUN TURF WAR?
WATER UNDER THE BRIDGE!
NO IT'S NO
ANYWAY I BROUGHT YOU HERE BECAUSE THE INVESTIGATION OF THE TEMPLE IMPORTED BY MY DEAR DEPARTED FATHER IS . . . NOT GOING WELL
. . . THAT THING IS YOURS?!
YES! AND I NEED TO KNOW WHAT'S IN THIS TEMPLE. MY FATHER'S NOTES ARE INCOMPLETE AND I NEED YOUR HELP TO FINISH THEM, GIVEN YOUR SPIRITUAL CONNECTION TO THE PLACE
HOW DO YOU KNOW ABOUT THAT?
A LITTLE BIRD TOLD ME
ALSO A RACCOON, A BOBCAT AND A CONVENT OF SQUIRREL-NUNS
SABRINA, EXPLAIN THE HAT THING
I CAN'T GET INTO DETAILS, BUT THE ONLY WAY ANYONE CAN GET INSIDE THE TEMPLE IN ITS CURRENT STATE IS THROUGH THE "ADVENTURE WINDOW"
FACE THE TEMPLE ON ITS OWN, TRAP-LADEN TERMS
THESE HATS HELP ESTABLISH A "POWER CHANNEL" WITH MY MASTER--THEY WILL BOOST AND AUGMENT OUR SKILLS
BETWEEN THE FIVE OF US, IT'S BEST TO DELEGATE THESE VARIOUS POWERS
DARYL, NATURALLY, WILL BE OUR FRONT MAN, OR "WARRI--
CAN'T DO IT
WHA--BUT YOU'RE
A TOTAL COWARD, YES'M
I'LL BE THE BEEFY FIGHTER!

I DUNNO ABOUT IT, BUT MY COUSIN WHO'S A COYOTE SHOWED ME HOW TO USE A BOW'N ARROW?
EEE
PERFECT!
I WAS EXPECTING THE FOX TO BE OUR THIEF, BUT YOU'LL HAVE TO DO
GOOD! AT LEAST THAT'S A RESPECTABLE CAREER!
THAT LEAVES YOU AS--
UGH, I DON'T WANT TO BE THE PRIEST OR HEALER OR WHATEVER! IF I GOTTA DO THIS, WHY DO I HAVE TO PLAY INTO THIS STUPID ROLE THAT I HATE?
AS THE HEALER, YOU'LL BE THE MOST CLOSELY PROTECTED OUT OF EVERYONE
GIMME THAT BIRETTA
STAY FROSTY GUYS, WE'RE HERE
KARI, IF YOU PLEASE?
OPEN . . . SESAME!
JUST OPEN THE DOOR YOU BIG IDJIT
RIGHT-O, SLINKY!
CLIK
WHAT'S THE BIG DEAL ANYHOW? I'VE BEEN INSIDE; IT'S A GIANT . . .
. . . ROOM?
I CALL DIBS ON SHINIES!
FOR THE LAST TIME, NO DIBS!
AS THIS IS AN EXPLORATORY MISSION, WE'LL COVER MORE GROUND IF WE--
NO
NEVER SPLIT THE PARTY!
NEED I REMIND YOU THAT YOU TASTE DELICIOUS TO VARIOUS, UNKNOWABLE ENTITIES?
NEED I REMIND YOU THAT I'M THE LEADER?
UGH, FINE! WELL DO IT THE SLOW WAY!
SNAP

KARI, LEAD US SOMEWHERE YOU HAVEN'T BEEN
WELL THERE'S BARCELONA, AND ZIMBABWE, AND--
SOMEWHERE IN HERE
HE'S BEEN IN HERE BY HIMSELF?
WHY DO YOU THINK I HAVE HIM ON MY PAYROLL? IT'S NOT SENTIMENTALITY I'LL TELL YOU THAT MUCH
I MEAN, HOW DID HE SURVIVE?
I DUNNO! I JUST POINT HIM IN A DIRECTION AND DON'T ASK QUESTIONS
BUT IF HE STILL HAS ALL HIS LIMBS, THIS PLACE CAN'T BE THAT DANGEROUS, RIGHT?
EEEEEEK
WHAT ARE THOSE?!
OH RIGHT, GARGOYLES
WE'D BETTER RUN
I DIDN'T DO IT!
CURSE MY LOVE OF LONG NARROW PASSAGES!
LISTEN! WE'LL START BY MAKING A BATTLE PERIMETER! DON'T LET YOURSELF BE SURROUND--
TELEPORT!
OR WE COULD DO THIS, YEAH
PIFF
WHY DIDN'T YOU TELL ME YOU COULD DO THAT?!
YOU KNOW NOW!
BESIDES, THERE'S LOTS OF THINGS YOU DON'T KNOW
THEN TELL ME EVERYTHING! THIS IS SORT OF CRITICAL!
WE'D BE IN MORE TROUBLE IF I TOLD YOU!
WE'LL BE FINE SO LONG AS WE STICK TOGETHER!
HA HA! YOUR MOTHERS WERE MADE OF CLAY AND YOUR FATHERS WERE MADE OF CHEESE!
. . . SPEAKING OF, WHERE DID ZACH GO?
UH-OH
I DON'T WANNA PLAY ANYMORE I DON'T WANNA PLAY ANYMORE I DON'T WANNA--
EEP!
MAYBE IF I SQUEEZE MY EYES SHUT NOTHING WILL EVER FIND ME FOREVER
IT IS PITCH BLACK. YOU ARE LIKELY TO BE EATEN BY A GRUE.
WHO SAID THAT

THE GRUE IS A SINISTER, LURKING PRESENCE IN THE DARK PLACES OF THE EARTH. ITS FAVORITE DIET IS ADVENTURERS, BUT ITS INSATIABLE APPETITE IS TEMPERED BY ITS FEAR OF LIGHT.
BUT I DON'T HAVE ANY LIGHT!
THAT REALLY IS TOO BAD
THUNK
HI THERE, YOU EVER PLAY CORNHOLE?
THE GRUE DISLIKES CORNHOLE AND MOVES INTO THE DARKER DARKNESS
NOW WHAT DO WE HAVE HERE?
CLIK
GASP!
WHAT HAVE I DONE? THEY'VE *KILLED* THE *WABBIT!*
I MEAN RABBIT
UM, I'M NOT DEAD
I KNOW, BUT I ALWAYS WANTED TO SAY THAT
YOU--YOU GUYS SURVIVED!
OF COURSE! YOU DIDN'T THINK I'D BRING YOU IN HERE UNPREPARED, DID YOU?
THE OPEN PIT GAVE US A BOTTLENECK; THEY COULDN'T ALL JUMP OVER AT ONCE
THE REST RETREATED BEFORE TOO LONG
AND FOR FUTURE REFERENCE, YOU *DO* HAVE A "LIGHT" SPELL. JUST CAST IT
CAST LIGHT?
AND WORK ON YOUR AIM
FOOSH
SAY, YOU'RE PRETTY LIGHT ON YOUR FEET!
WHAT'S THIS? CAN YOU READ IT?
NO. HOWEVER, I CAN VIEW THE TEXT ON THE ASTRAL PLANE, AND INTERPRET THE RAW INTENTIONS BEHIND THE WORDS INSTEAD
"O SEEKERS OF FORTUNE, LISTEN WELL. I SHALL DELIVER TO THE WHOLE WORLD A MARVELOUS GIFT, ONE I HAVE RARELY SEEN ON OTHER WORLDS
THIS PROMISE, THAT ONE DAY MAN AND BEAST WILL STAND SIDE BY SIDE"
"THOUGH IT WOULD TAKE ALL OF THE POWER I AM AFFORDED IN THIS WORLD, I WILL DO THIS THING IF YOU WOULD PLEASE, PLEASE, PLEASE, PLEASE, PLEASE MOVE THIS STUPID TEMPLE SOMEPLACE OTHER THAN A ME-FORSAKEN DESERT AAAARGH"
I MAY BE PARAPHRASING
YOU DON'T SAY

THERE'S ALSO FINE PRINT ABOUT HIM NEEDING TO SETTLE . . . ERM, SOME BUSINESS
BUT IT DOESN'T TELL US ANYTHING NEW!
THERE'S NO WHY, THERE'S NO HOW, THERE'S ONLY A DO THIS THING
IF THERE'S NO WAY TO CAPITALIZE ON THAT PROMISE, OR EVEN EVIDENCE IT CAN BE DONE, THEN THIS HAS BEEN A BIG WASTE OF--
CLIK...
AAACK
KROOM
HEY! I WAS SUPPOSED TO BE THE ONE WHO BUMBLES INTO TRAPS!
WE'RE JUST AS SURPRISED AS YOU
OH MY . . .
DOUBLOONS! TRIPLOONS!
I'LL BE A DINGO'S BABY, THAT'S GOTTA BE AN ENTIRE MINE'S WORTH OF GOLD
I'LL AGREE! IT IS ENTIRELY MINE
I'D SAY SOMETHING BUT FOR THE BLOOD RUSHING TO MY HEAD
PEOPLE, GRAB AS MUCH LOOT AS YOU CAN! WE NEED TO COMPARE THIS TO MY FATHER'S NOTES TO SEE IF--
THAT IS QUITE ENOUGH, MORTALS
SABRINA, PLEASE TELL ME THAT SOUL-DEADENING VOICE WAS ANOTHER ONE OF YOUR SPELLS
SORRY, PUNKIN. PLEASE PAY ATTENTION TO THE SOUL-DEADENING VOICE
NOT BAD EVERYONE. BUT THIS IS THE END OF THE LINE, YOU'RE ALL TOO INEXPERIENCED TO CONTINUE ANY FURTHER
EXCEPT FOR THE FOX, I DON'T KNOW HOW HE KEEPS GETTING IN HERE
SEND MY REGARDS TO TAROT AND DRAGON
WAIT! YOU'RE THAT SUPERBEING WHO MADE A PROMISE TO MY FATHER, RIGHT?
I'VE MADE A PROMISE, YES
BUT DO NOT PRESUME TO SPEAK OF SUCH MATTERS WHEN--
I WILL PRESUME TO SPEAK! MY FATHER'S LEGACY DID NOT DIE WITH HIM, SO DO YOU INTEND ON KEEPING YOUR WORD OR NOT?
HE'S RIGHT, PETE. LIES DO NOT BECOME A DEMIGOD
WHY DON'T YOU GO AHEAD AND TELL HIM, SABRINA?
YOU KNOW WHAT I MUST DO
. . . SABRINA, WHAT IS HE TALKING ABOUT?
. . . TWO THINGS
FIRST, HE CANNOT SURRENDER ALL HIS POWER AT ONCE TO DO THIS TASK, BECAUSE IT WOULD CAUSE HIM TO LOSE A BET WITH MY MASTER, WHICH WOULD CAUSE HIM TO LOSE SAID POWER ANYHOW
THAT WAS IN THE FINE PRINT
SECOND, HE IS AT ODDS WITH MY MASTER ON THIS MATTER. FORCING EQUALITY ON THE WORLD WOULD CREATE A CATASTROPHE
PETE PRESUMES THE HIGH PRICE IS WORTH IT, MY MASTER DOES NOT
YOUR MASTER IS TOO CODDLING OF YOU MORTALS
PAIN MAY PRECEDE CHANGE, BUT IN THE END, YOU MORTALS GET YOUR HAPPILY-EVER-AFTERS
HEY, THIS IS EXACTLY LIKE IN MY DREAMS!
I'LL SAY
1001 POULTRY RECIPES

ZACH: I didn't understand. Reconciling humans and animals? Bringing about a CATASTROPHE to do it? I thought we'd come to seek treasure, and instead we fell into an ongoing demigod drama... and, well, while I always took Keene as the kind of guy who'd make a deal with the devil, I didn't expect him to do it LITERALLY.

ALL HALLOW'S WEEN

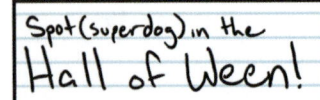

Panel 1: Spot (superdog) in the Hall of Ween! Gentlemen and gentle various-animals, Halloween is coming up, and you know what that means!

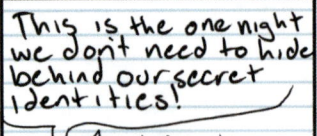

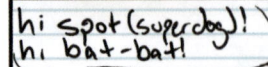

Panel 2: This is the one night we don't need to hide behind our secret identities!

Panel 3: hi spot (superdog)! hi bat-bat!
Hi kids! Haha, they don't know we're real!

Panel 4: Wait

Panel 5:
- So what are you gonna dress as for Halloween?
- I was thinking about a vampire

Panel 6:
- =PFFSH=
- What's wrong with vampires? I mean, as long as you stick to the traditional, Bela Lugosi style

Panel 7: You can't go as a vampire anymore--it's too generic! Halloween *used* to be about various genres of ghouls, but now it emphasizes how unique you can be

Panel 8:
- Is that why half of all boys dress as *Spider-Man*, and the other half as *Batman*?
- That's hardly accurate! The *Avengers* are also big this year

Panel 9: After their last adventure, a certain fox followed a certain black cat home and started, um, hanging out

Panel 10: *(no dialogue)*

Panel 11:
- You do know we have a stepladder for this sort of thing
- Oh I know, but those aren't self-propelled

Panel 12: To the hallway!

24

Panel 1: OOOH! I AM A GHOST! ≶TEE-HEE≶ / SASHA, THOSE ARE MY OWNER'S SHEETS SO *PLEASE* CUT IT OUT

Panel 2: (silent)

Panel 3: DON'T YOU START! I FOLDED IT OVER TWICE SO THE EYEHOLES WOULD BE EVEN!

Panel 4: (silent)

Panel 5: BLARG IMMA EAT YOU / AAAAH!

Panel 6: OKAY GOOD! ON A SCALE OF ONE TO FIVE, HOW SCARED WOULD YOU SAY YOU WERE? REMEMBER, HONESTY IMPROVES YOUR HALLOWEEN EXPERIENCE / I THINK MY HEART EXPLODED / I'LL MARK THAT AS A "4"

25

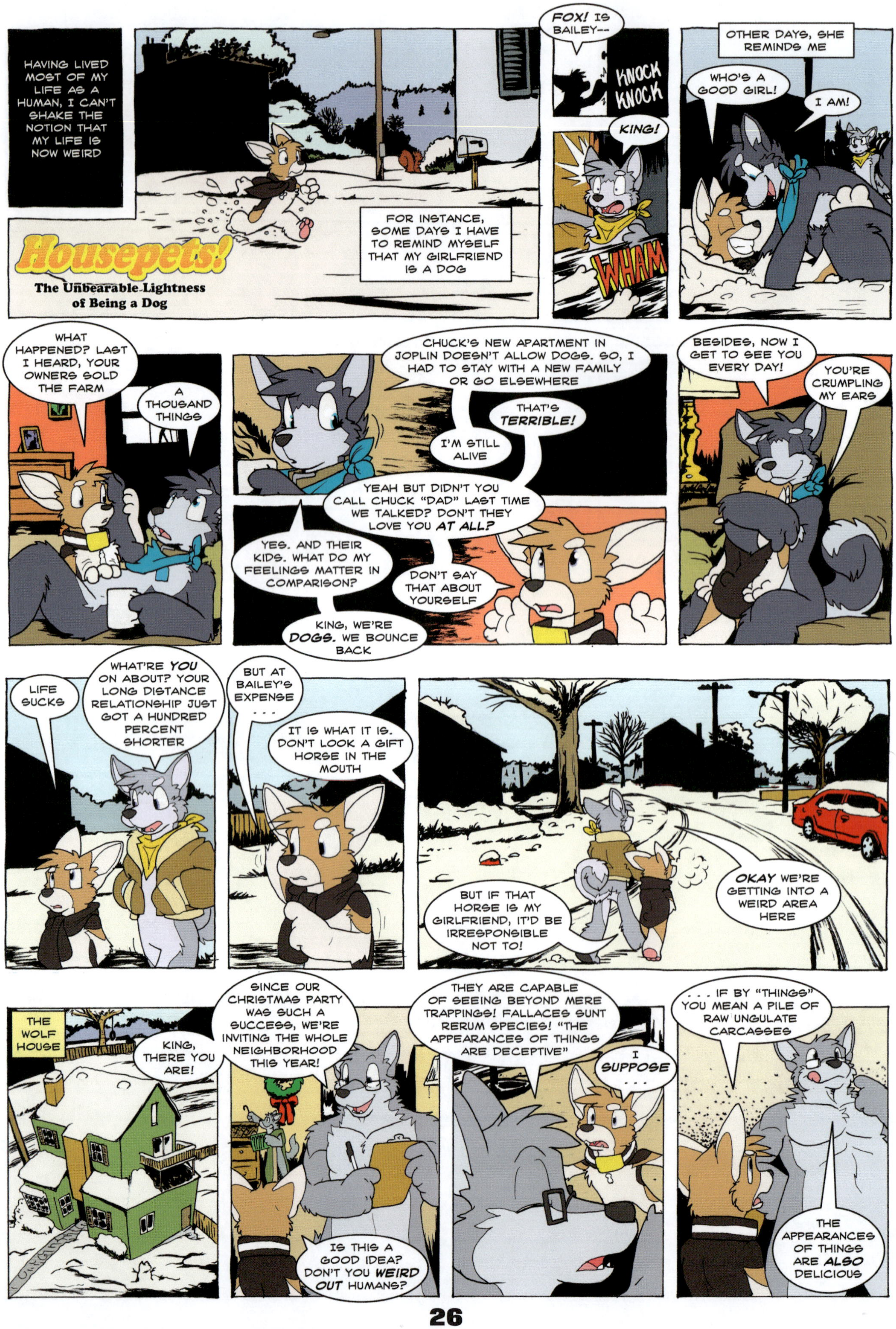
HAVING LIVED MOST OF MY LIFE AS A HUMAN, I CAN'T SHAKE THE NOTION THAT MY LIFE IS NOW WEIRD
Housepets!
The Unbearable Lightness of Being a Dog
FOR INSTANCE, SOME DAYS I HAVE TO REMIND MYSELF THAT MY GIRLFRIEND IS A DOG
FOX! IS BAILEY--
KNOCK KNOCK
KING!
WHAM
OTHER DAYS, SHE REMINDS ME
WHO'S A GOOD GIRL!
I AM!
WHAT HAPPENED? LAST I HEARD, YOUR OWNERS SOLD THE FARM
A THOUSAND THINGS
CHUCK'S NEW APARTMENT IN JOPLIN DOESN'T ALLOW DOGS. SO, I HAD TO STAY WITH A NEW FAMILY OR GO ELSEWHERE
I'M STILL ALIVE
THAT'S TERRIBLE!
YEAH BUT DIDN'T YOU CALL CHUCK "DAD" LAST TIME WE TALKED? DON'T THEY LOVE YOU AT ALL?
YES. AND THEIR KIDS. WHAT DO MY FEELINGS MATTER IN COMPARISON?
DON'T SAY THAT ABOUT YOURSELF
KING, WE'RE DOGS. WE BOUNCE BACK
BESIDES, NOW I GET TO SEE YOU EVERY DAY!
YOU'RE CRUMPLING MY EARS
LIFE SUCKS
WHAT'RE YOU ON ABOUT? YOUR LONG DISTANCE RELATIONSHIP JUST GOT A HUNDRED PERCENT SHORTER
BUT AT BAILEY'S EXPENSE . . .
IT IS WHAT IT IS. DON'T LOOK A GIFT HORSE IN THE MOUTH
BUT IF THAT HORSE IS MY GIRLFRIEND, IT'D BE IRRESPONSIBLE NOT TO!
OKAY WE'RE GETTING INTO A WEIRD AREA HERE
THE WOLF HOUSE
KING, THERE YOU ARE!
SINCE OUR CHRISTMAS PARTY WAS SUCH A SUCCESS, WE'RE INVITING THE WHOLE NEIGHBORHOOD THIS YEAR!
IS THIS A GOOD IDEA? DON'T YOU WEIRD OUT HUMANS?
THEY ARE CAPABLE OF SEEING BEYOND MERE TRAPPINGS! FALLACES SUNT RERUM SPECIES! "THE APPEARANCES OF THINGS ARE DECEPTIVE"
I SUPPOSE . . .
. . . IF BY "THINGS" YOU MEAN A PILE OF RAW UNGULATE CARCASSES
THE APPEARANCES OF THINGS ARE ALSO DELICIOUS

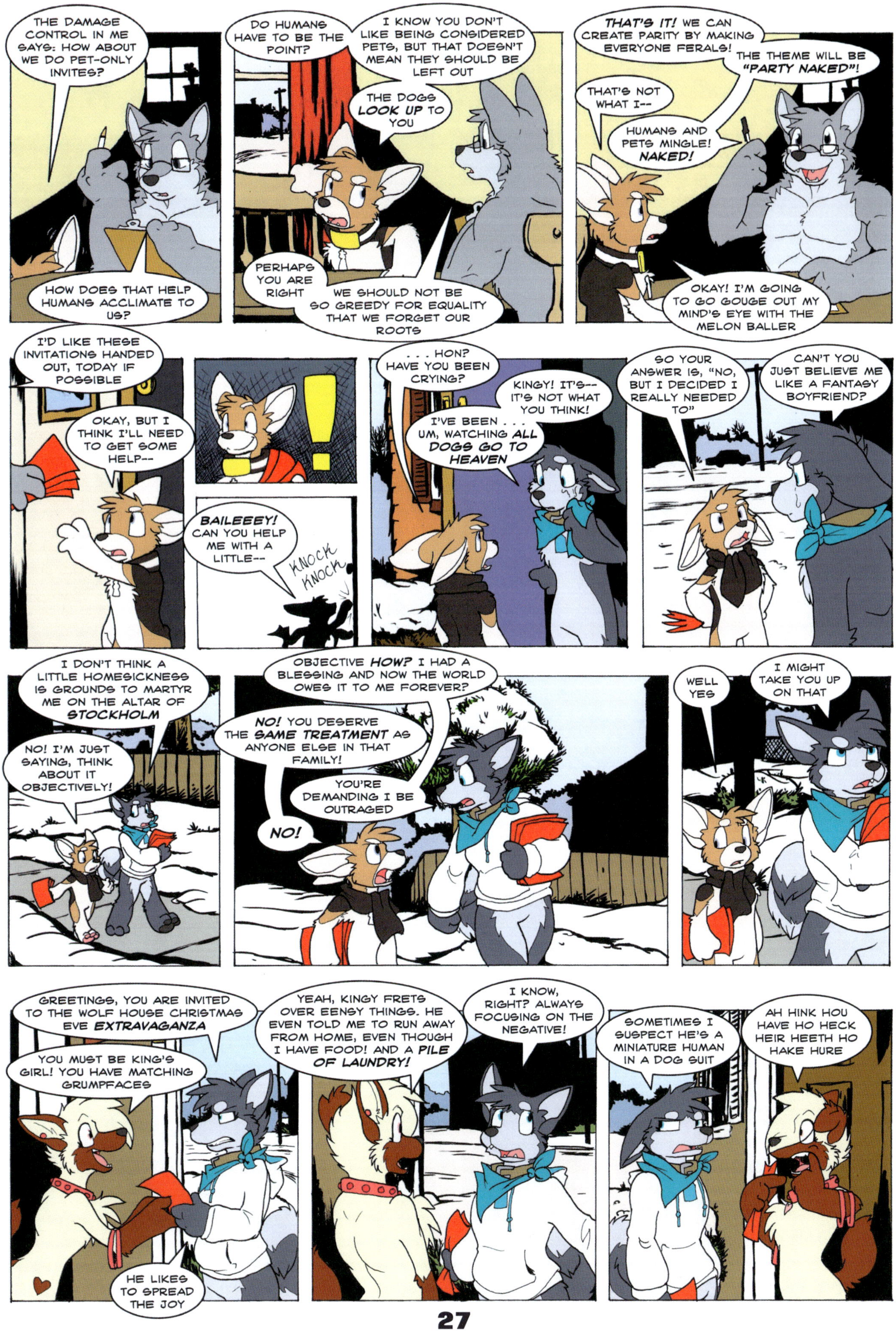
THE DAMAGE CONTROL IN ME SAYS: HOW ABOUT WE DO PET-ONLY INVITES?
HOW DOES THAT HELP HUMANS ACCLIMATE TO US?
DO HUMANS HAVE TO BE THE POINT?
I KNOW YOU DON'T LIKE BEING CONSIDERED PETS, BUT THAT DOESN'T MEAN THEY SHOULD BE LEFT OUT
THE DOGS LOOK UP TO YOU
PERHAPS YOU ARE RIGHT
WE SHOULD NOT BE SO GREEDY FOR EQUALITY THAT WE FORGET OUR ROOTS
THAT'S IT! WE CAN CREATE PARITY BY MAKING EVERYONE FERALS!
THE THEME WILL BE "PARTY NAKED"!
THAT'S NOT WHAT I--
HUMANS AND PETS MINGLE! NAKED!
OKAY! I'M GOING TO GO GOUGE OUT MY MIND'S EYE WITH THE MELON BALLER
I'D LIKE THESE INVITATIONS HANDED OUT, TODAY IF POSSIBLE
OKAY, BUT I THINK I'LL NEED TO GET SOME HELP--
!
BAILEEEY! CAN YOU HELP ME WITH A LITTLE--
KNOCK KNOCK
. . . HON? HAVE YOU BEEN CRYING?
KINGY! IT'S-- IT'S NOT WHAT YOU THINK!
I'VE BEEN . . . UM, WATCHING ALL DOGS GO TO HEAVEN
SO YOUR ANSWER IS, "NO, BUT I DECIDED I REALLY NEEDED TO"
CAN'T YOU JUST BELIEVE ME LIKE A FANTASY BOYFRIEND?
I DON'T THINK A LITTLE HOMESICKNESS IS GROUNDS TO MARTYR ME ON THE ALTAR OF STOCKHOLM
NO! I'M JUST SAYING, THINK ABOUT IT OBJECTIVELY!
OBJECTIVE HOW? I HAD A BLESSING AND NOW THE WORLD OWES IT TO ME FOREVER?
NO! YOU DESERVE THE SAME TREATMENT AS ANYONE ELSE IN THAT FAMILY!
YOU'RE DEMANDING I BE OUTRAGED
NO!
WELL YES
I MIGHT TAKE YOU UP ON THAT
GREETINGS, YOU ARE INVITED TO THE WOLF HOUSE CHRISTMAS EVE EXTRAVAGANZA
YOU MUST BE KING'S GIRL! YOU HAVE MATCHING GRUMPFACES
HE LIKES TO SPREAD THE JOY
YEAH, KINGY FRETS OVER EENSY THINGS. HE EVEN TOLD ME TO RUN AWAY FROM HOME, EVEN THOUGH I HAVE FOOD! AND A PILE OF LAUNDRY!
I KNOW, RIGHT? ALWAYS FOCUSING ON THE NEGATIVE!
SOMETIMES I SUSPECT HE'S A MINIATURE HUMAN IN A DOG SUIT
AH HINK HOU HAVE HO HECK HEIR HEETH HO HAKE HURE

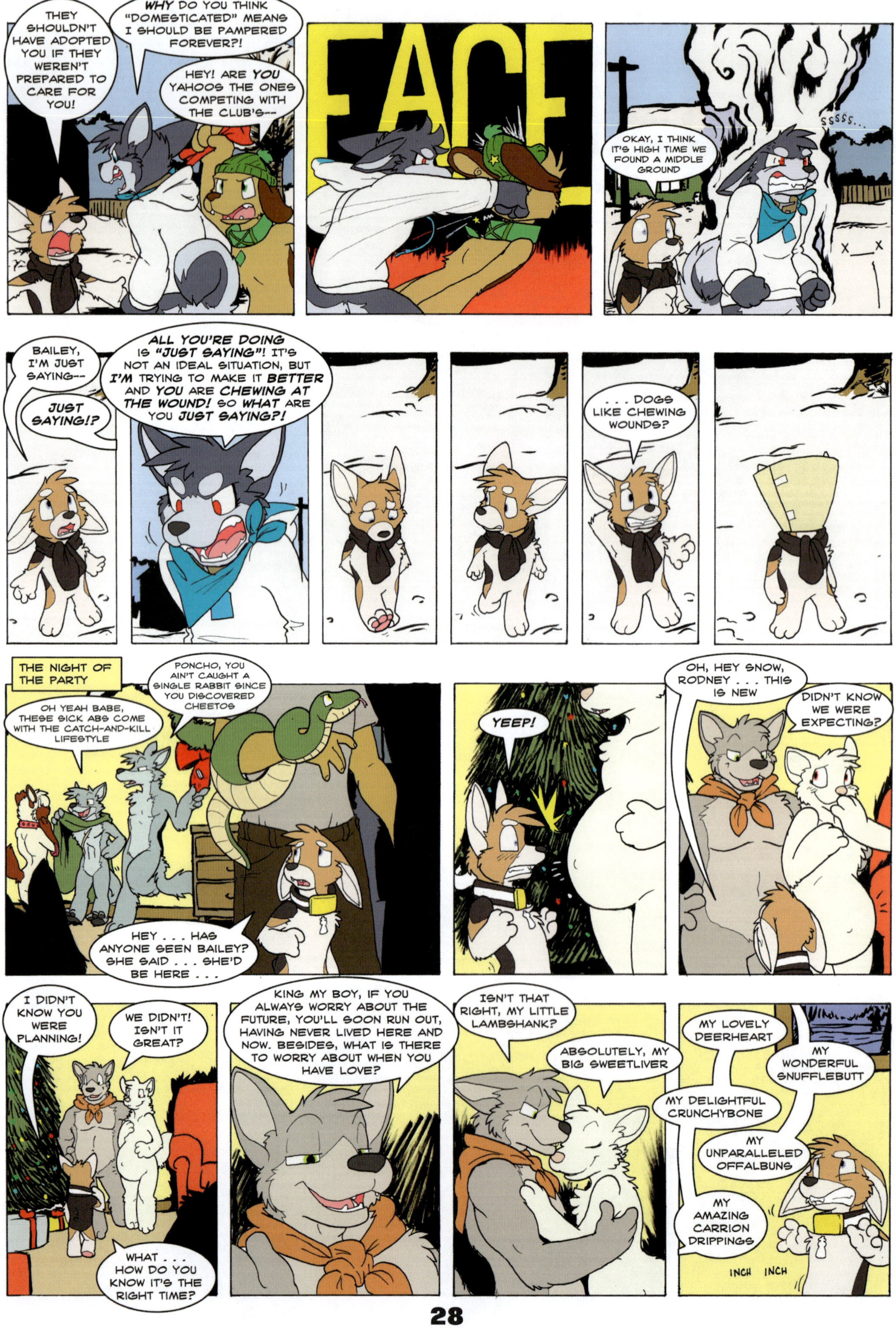
THEY SHOULDN'T HAVE ADOPTED YOU IF THEY WEREN'T PREPARED TO CARE FOR YOU!
WHY DO YOU THINK "DOMESTICATED" MEANS I SHOULD BE PAMPERED FOREVER?!
HEY! ARE YOU YAHOOS THE ONES COMPETING WITH THE CLUB'S--
FACE
OKAY, I THINK IT'S HIGH TIME WE FOUND A MIDDLE GROUND
SSSSS...
BAILEY, I'M JUST SAYING--
JUST SAYING!?
ALL YOU'RE DOING IS "JUST SAYING"! IT'S NOT AN IDEAL SITUATION, BUT I'M TRYING TO MAKE IT BETTER AND YOU ARE CHEWING AT THE WOUND! SO WHAT ARE YOU JUST SAYING?!
. . . DOGS LIKE CHEWING WOUNDS?
THE NIGHT OF THE PARTY
OH YEAH BABE, THESE SICK ABS COME WITH THE CATCH-AND-KILL LIFESTYLE
PONCHO, YOU AIN'T CAUGHT A SINGLE RABBIT SINCE YOU DISCOVERED CHEETOS
HEY . . . HAS ANYONE SEEN BAILEY? SHE SAID . . . SHE'D BE HERE . . .
YEEP!
OH, HEY SNOW, RODNEY . . . THIS IS NEW
DIDN'T KNOW WE WERE EXPECTING?
I DIDN'T KNOW YOU WERE PLANNING!
WE DIDN'T! ISN'T IT GREAT?
WHAT . . . HOW DO YOU KNOW IT'S THE RIGHT TIME?
KING MY BOY, IF YOU ALWAYS WORRY ABOUT THE FUTURE, YOU'LL SOON RUN OUT, HAVING NEVER LIVED HERE AND NOW. BESIDES, WHAT IS THERE TO WORRY ABOUT WHEN YOU HAVE LOVE?
ISN'T THAT RIGHT, MY LITTLE LAMBSHANK?
ABSOLUTELY, MY BIG SWEETLIVER
MY LOVELY DEERHEART
MY WONDERFUL SNUFFLEBUTT
MY DELIGHTFUL CRUNCHYBONE
MY UNPARALLELED OFFALBUNS
MY AMAZING CARRION DRIPPINGS
INCH INCH

I SAW WHO WAS COMING UP THE WALK BEHIND ME
GOOD TO SEE YOU, BIGGLESWORTH! AND YOUR MOTHER CAME TOO!
YOU DID TELL HER WE WERE DROPPING THE AU NATURALE THEME, RIGHT?
CAN WE TALK SOMEWHERE PRIVATE?
WHAT'S WRONG WITH HERE?
IF THE GUEST COATS ARE IN THE HALL, THEN WHAT ARE ALL THESE--
I'VE LEARNED NOT TO ASK QUESTIONS
GET OUT
YESSIR
BUT THE PAWS!
FOR THE LAST TIME, YOU CAN'T RUN AROUND ON THE FLOOR!
KCHNG
HI I'M DAISY!
WELL AT LEAST NOTHING ON THE PORCH CAN INTERRUPT US
HEY! MISTLETOE!
YOU DIDN'T SEE ANYTHING
HAS ANYONE SEEN OFFICER FIDO? HE'S BEEN ACTING WEIRD
YOU'RE NOT STILL UPSET?
OF COURSE NOT! I KNOW YOU MEANT WELL, AND YOU MEAN MORE TO ME THAN BICKERING COULD EVER RUIN
THAT'S GOING TO MAKE THIS A LOT LESS AWKWARD THEN
WHAT'S THIS?
BAILEY, WILL YOU MARRY ME?

KING, ARE YOU CRAZY?! WHAT ARE YOU TRYING TO PROVE? IT'S NOT LIKE ANYONE TAKES "PET MARRIAGES" SERIOUSLY!
BUT I AM SERIOUS
I DON'T EXPECT YOU TO SAY YES. I HAVE FLAWS AND MAKE STUPID MISTAKES
I WANT TO DO THIS RIGHT--TO MAKE THINGS BETTER AND NOT WORSE. PUT ASIDE WHAT OTHER PEOPLE THINK. WOULD YOU WANT WHAT I'M OFFERING?
YOU GOT ME
YES!
HEY WAIT! I NEVER GOT TO SNIFF YOUR BUTT!
Merry Christmas! Rick Griffin
DO WE HAVE TO DO THIS NOW?!

Panel 1:
- I'LL TRADE FOUR SNACKERDOODLES FOR THE CINNA-NOMS
- THEY'RE WORTH MORE THAN THAT! TAKE THE CHEESE SNORKELS TOO

Panel 2:
- BLEGH. I GUESS I COULD GIVE THEM TO MAX
- YOU HAVE ANY *GENERIC FRUIT PIES?*
- ONLY IN BARBECUE FLAVOR

Panel 3:
- JUNK FOODS HAVEN'T BEEN THE SAME SINCE HOSTESS WENT UNDER
- HAS LITTLE DEBBIE ALWAYS HAD TWO CHINS?

Panel 4:
- JUST WHEN I THOUGHT IT COULDN'T GET ANY WORSE! I'M GONNA GIVE THE TEAMSTERS A PIECE OF MY MIND!

Panel 5:
- HOW CAN WE HAVE AN ELABORATE BIGGER-THAN-TIMES-SQUARE SETUP FOR NEW YEAR'S WHEN THESE SCREWUPS LOSE THE MOST IMPORTANT PIECE IN TRANSIT?!

Panel 6:
- I GUESS YOU COULD SAY THEY REALLY DROPPED TH—
- NO

Panel 8: CRINKLE

Panel 10:
- IT'S NOT A TREAT, PEANUT, IT'S JUST SOME WET WIPES
- YOU'VE LIED BEFORE!

Panel 11: SNIFF SNUF

Panel 12: SNF SNOOF SNEFF NOSE

Panel 13: SNEEF SNOF SNIFF SNOF SNF SNUF SNF SNIFF SNUF SNOOF SNOF SNEEF SNAF SF

Panel 14: VERY WELL...

Panel 15: NOSE SNIFF SNUF

Panel 16: SNERRRRK NIP NIP

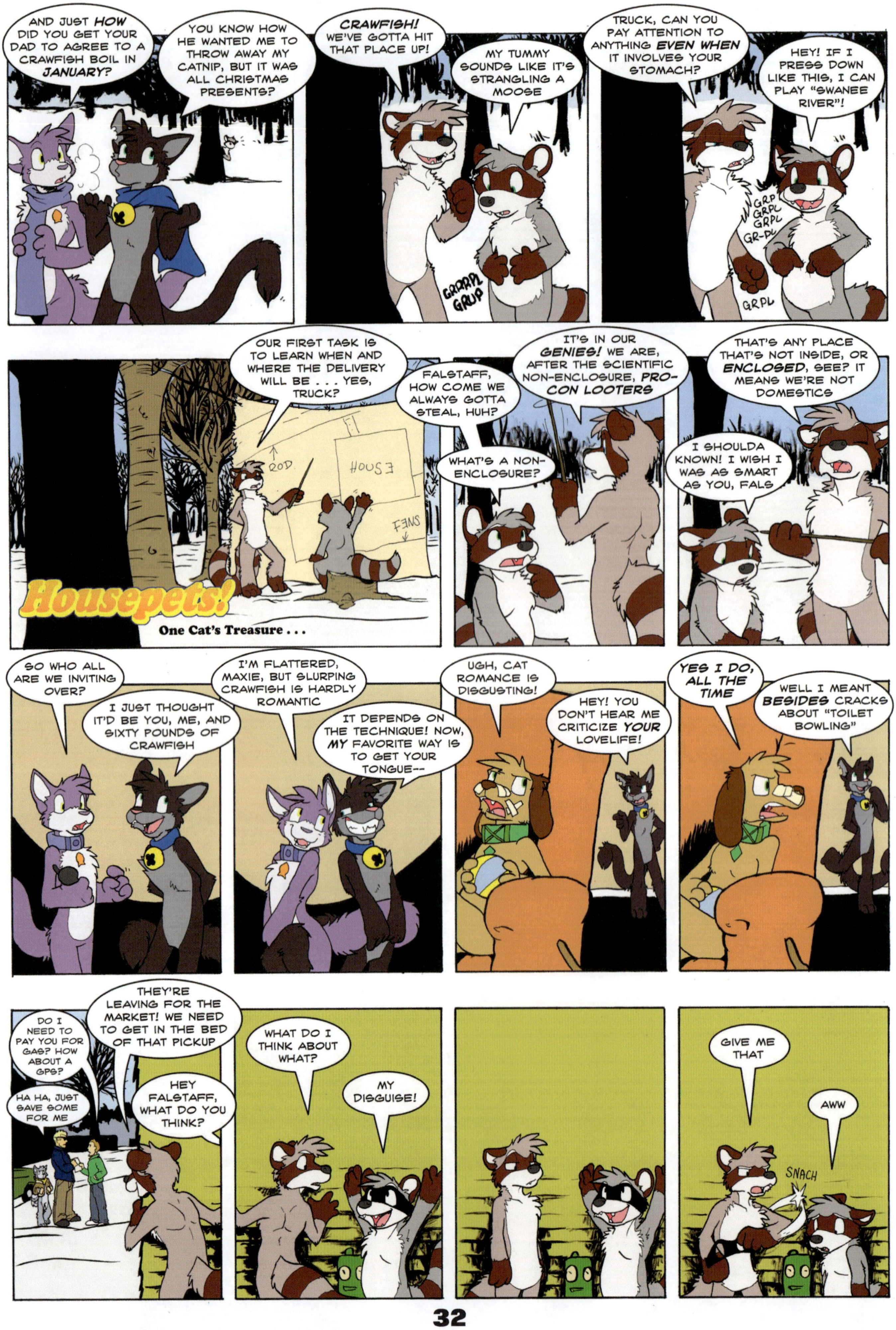

AND JUST HOW DID YOU GET YOUR DAD TO AGREE TO A CRAWFISH BOIL IN JANUARY?
YOU KNOW HOW HE WANTED ME TO THROW AWAY MY CATNIP, BUT IT WAS ALL CHRISTMAS PRESENTS?
CRAWFISH! WE'VE GOTTA HIT THAT PLACE UP!
MY TUMMY SOUNDS LIKE IT'S STRANGLING A MOOSE
GRRRPL GRUP
TRUCK, CAN YOU PAY ATTENTION TO ANYTHING EVEN WHEN IT INVOLVES YOUR STOMACH?
HEY! IF I PRESS DOWN LIKE THIS, I CAN PLAY "SWANEE RIVER"!
GRP GRPL GRPL GR-PL
GRPL
OUR FIRST TASK IS TO LEARN WHEN AND WHERE THE DELIVERY WILL BE . . . YES, TRUCK?
ROD.
HOUSE
FENS
Housepets!
One Cat's Treasure . . .
FALSTAFF, HOW COME WE ALWAYS GOTTA STEAL, HUH?
IT'S IN OUR GENIES! WE ARE, AFTER THE SCIENTIFIC NON-ENCLOSURE, PRO-CON LOOTERS
WHAT'S A NON-ENCLOSURE?
THAT'S ANY PLACE THAT'S NOT INSIDE, OR ENCLOSED, SEE? IT MEANS WE'RE NOT DOMESTICS
I SHOULDA KNOWN! I WISH I WAS AS SMART AS YOU, FALS
SO WHO ALL ARE WE INVITING OVER?
I JUST THOUGHT IT'D BE YOU, ME, AND SIXTY POUNDS OF CRAWFISH
I'M FLATTERED, MAXIE, BUT SLURPING CRAWFISH IS HARDLY ROMANTIC
IT DEPENDS ON THE TECHNIQUE! NOW, MY FAVORITE WAY IS TO GET YOUR TONGUE--
UGH, CAT ROMANCE IS DISGUSTING!
HEY! YOU DON'T HEAR ME CRITICIZE YOUR LOVELIFE!
YES I DO, ALL THE TIME
WELL I MEANT BESIDES CRACKS ABOUT "TOILET BOWLING"
DO I NEED TO PAY YOU FOR GAS? HOW ABOUT A GPS?
HA HA, JUST SAVE SOME FOR ME
THEY'RE LEAVING FOR THE MARKET! WE NEED TO GET IN THE BED OF THAT PICKUP
HEY FALSTAFF, WHAT DO YOU THINK?
WHAT DO I THINK ABOUT WHAT?
MY DISGUISE!
GIVE ME THAT
SNACH
AWW

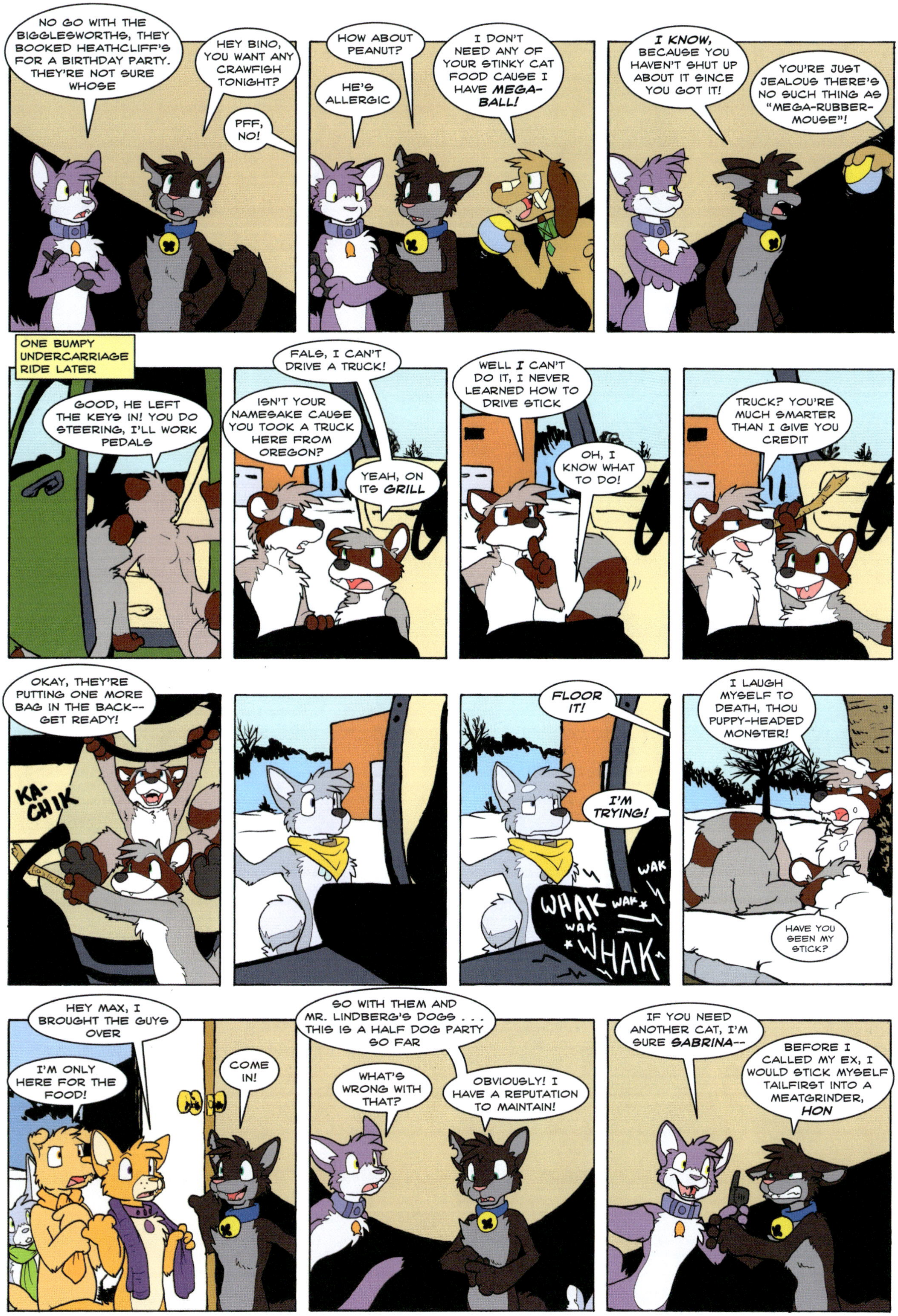
NO GO WITH THE BIGGLESWORTHS, THEY BOOKED HEATHCLIFF'S FOR A BIRTHDAY PARTY. THEY'RE NOT SURE WHOSE
HEY BINO, YOU WANT ANY CRAWFISH TONIGHT?
PFF, NO!
HOW ABOUT PEANUT?
HE'S ALLERGIC
I DON'T NEED ANY OF YOUR STINKY CAT FOOD CAUSE I HAVE MEGA-BALL!
I KNOW, BECAUSE YOU HAVEN'T SHUT UP ABOUT IT SINCE YOU GOT IT!
YOU'RE JUST JEALOUS THERE'S NO SUCH THING AS "MEGA-RUBBER-MOUSE"!
ONE BUMPY UNDERCARRIAGE RIDE LATER
GOOD, HE LEFT THE KEYS IN! YOU DO STEERING, I'LL WORK PEDALS
FALS, I CAN'T DRIVE A TRUCK!
ISN'T YOUR NAMESAKE CAUSE YOU TOOK A TRUCK HERE FROM OREGON?
YEAH, ON ITS GRILL
WELL I CAN'T DO IT, I NEVER LEARNED HOW TO DRIVE STICK
OH, I KNOW WHAT TO DO!
TRUCK? YOU'RE MUCH SMARTER THAN I GIVE YOU CREDIT
OKAY, THEY'RE PUTTING ONE MORE BAG IN THE BACK-- GET READY!
KA-CHIK
FLOOR IT!
I'M TRYING!
WHAK WAK WAK WAK WHAK
I LAUGH MYSELF TO DEATH, THOU PUPPY-HEADED MONSTER!
HAVE YOU SEEN MY STICK?
HEY MAX, I BROUGHT THE GUYS OVER
I'M ONLY HERE FOR THE FOOD!
COME IN!
SO WITH THEM AND MR. LINDBERG'S DOGS . . . THIS IS A HALF DOG PARTY SO FAR
WHAT'S WRONG WITH THAT?
OBVIOUSLY! I HAVE A REPUTATION TO MAINTAIN!
IF YOU NEED ANOTHER CAT, I'M SURE SABRINA--
BEFORE I CALLED MY EX, I WOULD STICK MYSELF TAILFIRST INTO A MEATGRINDER, HON

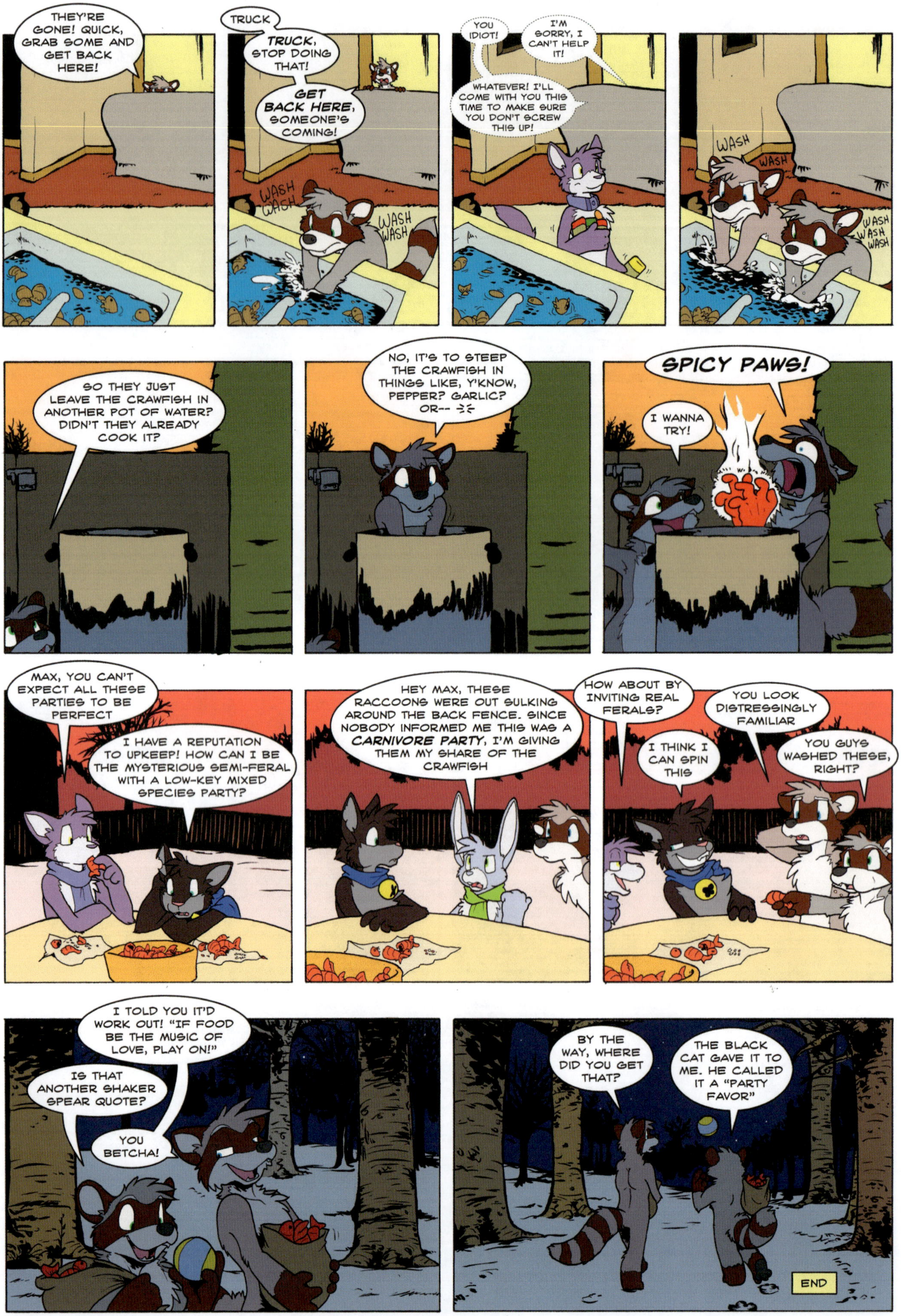
THEY'RE GONE! QUICK, GRAB SOME AND GET BACK HERE!
TRUCK
TRUCK, STOP DOING THAT!
GET BACK HERE, SOMEONE'S COMING!
WASH WASH
WASH WASH
YOU IDIOT!
I'M SORRY, I CAN'T HELP IT!
WHATEVER! I'LL COME WITH YOU THIS TIME TO MAKE SURE YOU DON'T SCREW THIS UP!
WASH
WASH
WASH WASH WASH
SO THEY JUST LEAVE THE CRAWFISH IN ANOTHER POT OF WATER? DIDN'T THEY ALREADY COOK IT?
NO, IT'S TO STEEP THE CRAWFISH IN THINGS LIKE, Y'KNOW, PEPPER? GARLIC? OR--
SPICY PAWS!
I WANNA TRY!
MAX, YOU CAN'T EXPECT ALL THESE PARTIES TO BE PERFECT
I HAVE A REPUTATION TO UPKEEP! HOW CAN I BE THE MYSTERIOUS SEMI-FERAL WITH A LOW-KEY MIXED SPECIES PARTY?
HEY MAX, THESE RACCOONS WERE OUT SULKING AROUND THE BACK FENCE. SINCE NOBODY INFORMED ME THIS WAS A CARNIVORE PARTY, I'M GIVING THEM MY SHARE OF THE CRAWFISH
HOW ABOUT BY INVITING REAL FERALS?
I THINK I CAN SPIN THIS
YOU LOOK DISTRESSINGLY FAMILIAR
YOU GUYS WASHED THESE, RIGHT?
I TOLD YOU IT'D WORK OUT! "IF FOOD BE THE MUSIC OF LOVE, PLAY ON!"
IS THAT ANOTHER SHAKER SPEAR QUOTE?
YOU BETCHA!
BY THE WAY, WHERE DID YOU GET THAT?
THE BLACK CAT GAVE IT TO ME. HE CALLED IT A "PARTY FAVOR"
END

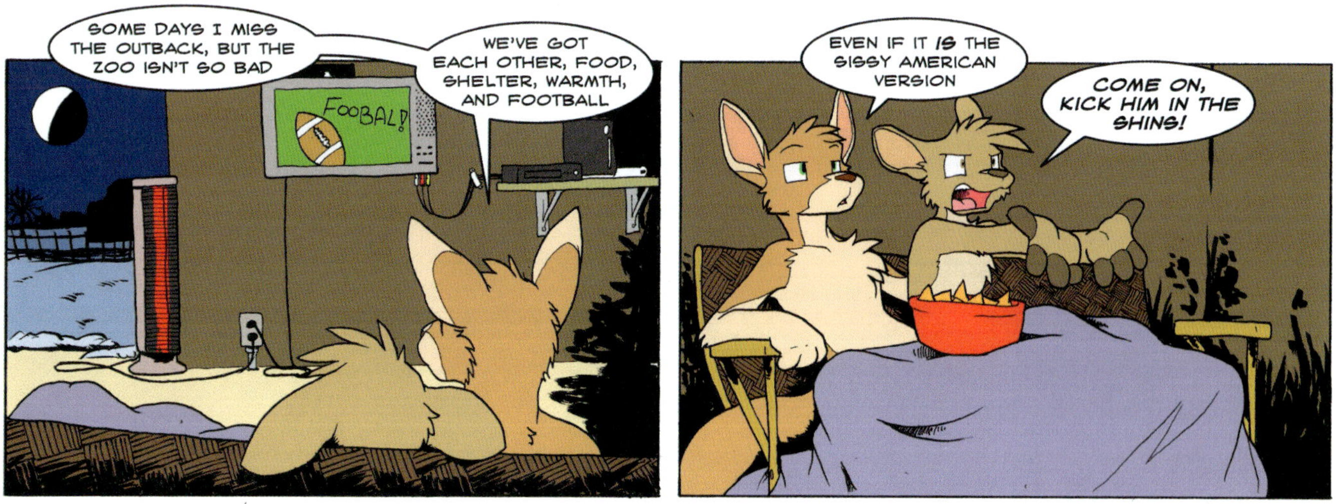

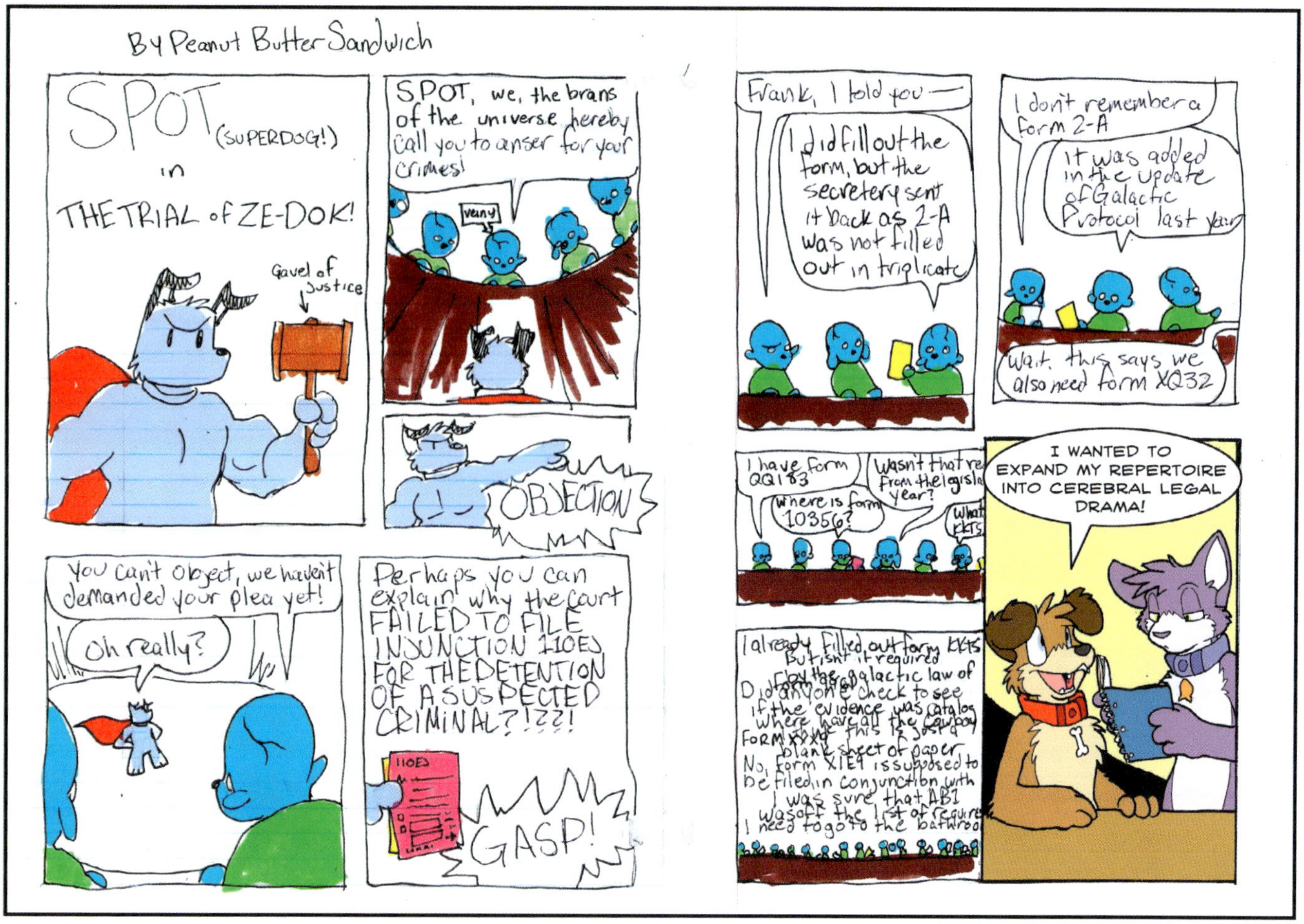

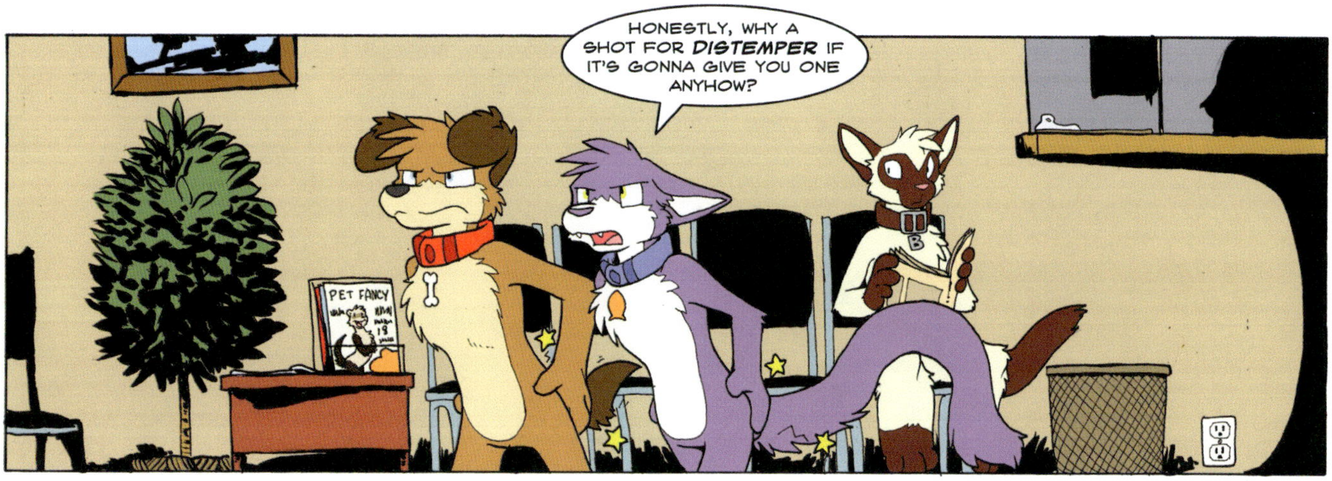

I'M JUST SURPRISED YOU SCHEDULED YOUR VALENTINE'S DATE ON, YOU KNOW, VALENTINES
FOX, YOU BOTHER ME WITH YOUR MOUTH SOMETIMES
I'M SERIOUS! IT'S LIKE YOU'RE FINALLY GROWING UP!
YOU'D UNDERSTAND IF YOU HAD A GIRLFRIEND--RELATIONSHIPS AREN'T ABOUT TRIVIAL THINGS, LIKE FLOWERS OR PRESENTS
IT'S ABOUT ANTICIPATING YOUR PARTNER'S WANTS AND DESIRES
Housepets!
Love And War
AND WHAT'S THE MOVIE YOU PICKED OUT FOR SASHA?
"SCREAMING BLOOD CULT VI", WHY?
BINEY!
SASH . . . Y
I GOT YOU A PRESENT!
SO DID I!
I MEAN, THAT I GOT YOU A PRESENT, NOT THAT YOU GOT ME A PRESENT, CAUSE YOU ALREADY--
YES I GOT IT
LET'S SHOW OUR PRESENTS ON THREE!
IF YOU WANT! YOU COUNT, YOU'RE BETTER AT IT
OKAY! ONE, TWO, THREE!
WHITE CHOCOLATE!
A DEAR JOHN LETTER!
WHAT
"DEAR JOHN"-- OOPS! I MEAN BINO! TEE-HEE
BINO, IT'S . . . PROBABLY NOT AS HORRIBLE AS IT SEEMS?
YOU'VE BROKEN UP BEFORE
US MAIL
BUT SHE WANTS TO DATE OTHER DOGS, NOT JUST MY BROTHER!
AND FIDO DIDN'T CARE, HE PROBABLY HAS . . . TENS . . . OF GIRLS! IT WAS A PREDICTABLE CYCLE!
BINO . . . ARE YOU SCARED YOU'RE NOT GOOD ENOUGH FOR HER TO COME BACK?
SIGH YEAH . . .
. . . WHICH IS WHY EVERYONE ELSE NEEDS TO MAKE ME LOOK GOOD BY COMPARISON!
I NEED TO STOP THROWING YOU PEARLS
GUYS, I REGRET TO INFORM YOU OF BINO'S PLAN
WE ARE GOING TO TURN A CORNER OF THE CLUBHOUSE INTO A COZY DINNER SETTING SO WE CAN ALL GO ON DATES WITH SASHA
WOO YEAH!
--AND INTENTIONALLY SABOTAGE THOSE DATES TO MAKE BINO LOOK BETTER
AWW, WHAT!
SO, WHAT, WE GOTS TA SALVAGE BINO'S RELATIONSHIP, WHEN WE AIN'T EVEN GOTS ANY GIRLS OF OUR OWN?!
SO WHAT YOU'RE SAYING IS, YOU DON'T HAVE ANYTHING TO DO FOR VALENTINES?
YEAH

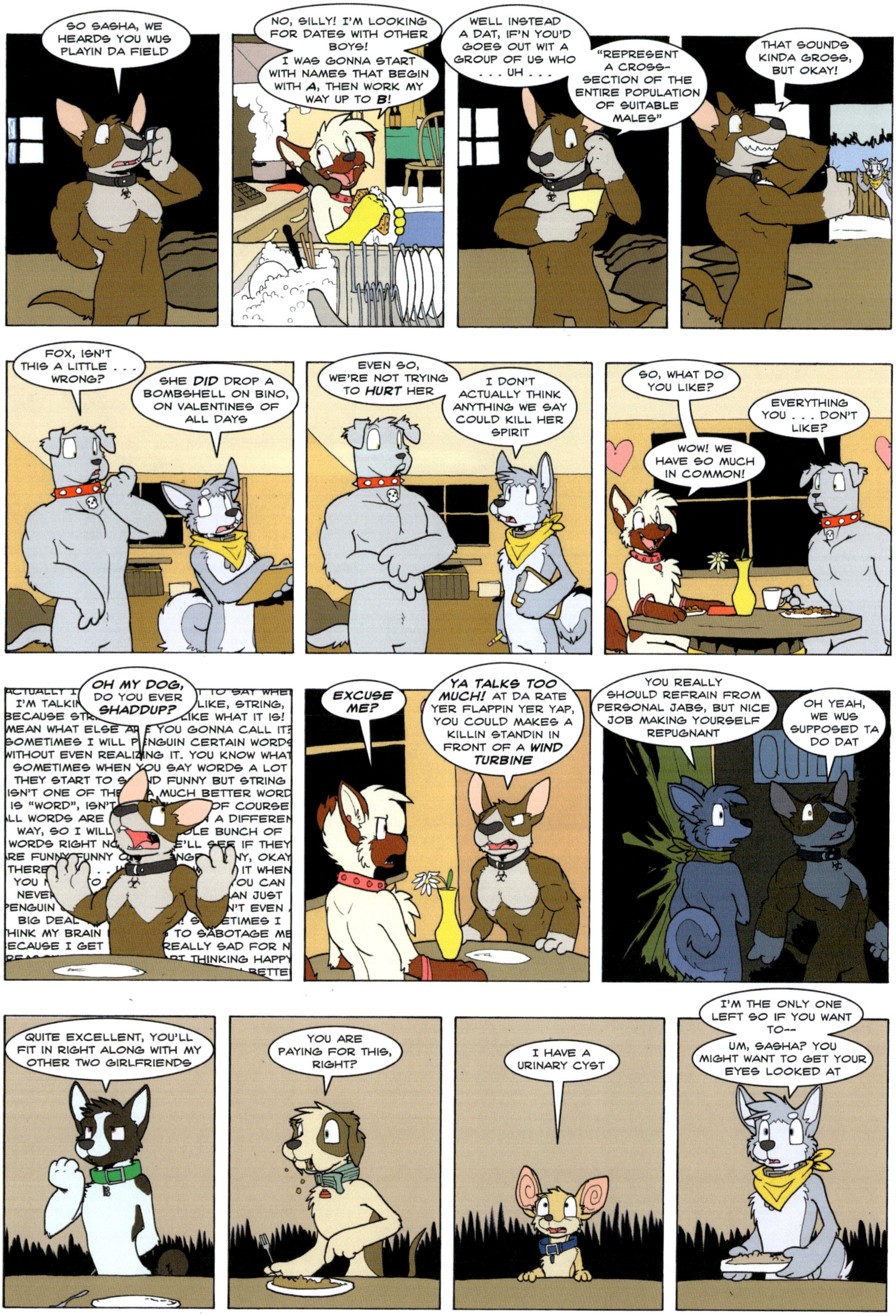
SO SASHA, WE HEARDS YOU WUS PLAYIN DA FIELD
NO, SILLY! I'M LOOKING FOR DATES WITH OTHER BOYS!
I WAS GONNA START WITH NAMES THAT BEGIN WITH A, THEN WORK MY WAY UP TO B!
WELL INSTEAD A DAT, IF'N YOU'D GOES OUT WIT A GROUP OF US WHO . . . UH . . .
"REPRESENT A CROSS-SECTION OF THE ENTIRE POPULATION OF SUITABLE MALES"
THAT SOUNDS KINDA GROSS, BUT OKAY!
FOX, ISN'T THIS A LITTLE . . . WRONG?
SHE DID DROP A BOMBSHELL ON BINO, ON VALENTINES OF ALL DAYS
EVEN SO, WE'RE NOT TRYING TO HURT HER
I DON'T ACTUALLY THINK ANYTHING WE SAY COULD KILL HER SPIRIT
SO, WHAT DO YOU LIKE?
EVERYTHING YOU . . . DON'T LIKE?
WOW! WE HAVE SO MUCH IN COMMON!
OH MY DOG, DO YOU EVER SHADDUP?
EXCUSE ME?
YA TALKS TOO MUCH! AT DA RATE YER FLAPPIN YER YAP, YOU COULD MAKES A KILLIN STANDIN IN FRONT OF A WIND TURBINE
YOU REALLY SHOULD REFRAIN FROM PERSONAL JABS, BUT NICE JOB MAKING YOURSELF REPUGNANT
OH YEAH, WE WUS SUPPOSED TA DO DAT
QUITE EXCELLENT, YOU'LL FIT IN RIGHT ALONG WITH MY OTHER TWO GIRLFRIENDS
YOU ARE PAYING FOR THIS, RIGHT?
I HAVE A URINARY CYST
I'M THE ONLY ONE LEFT SO IF YOU WANT TO--
UM, SASHA? YOU MIGHT WANT TO GET YOUR EYES LOOKED AT

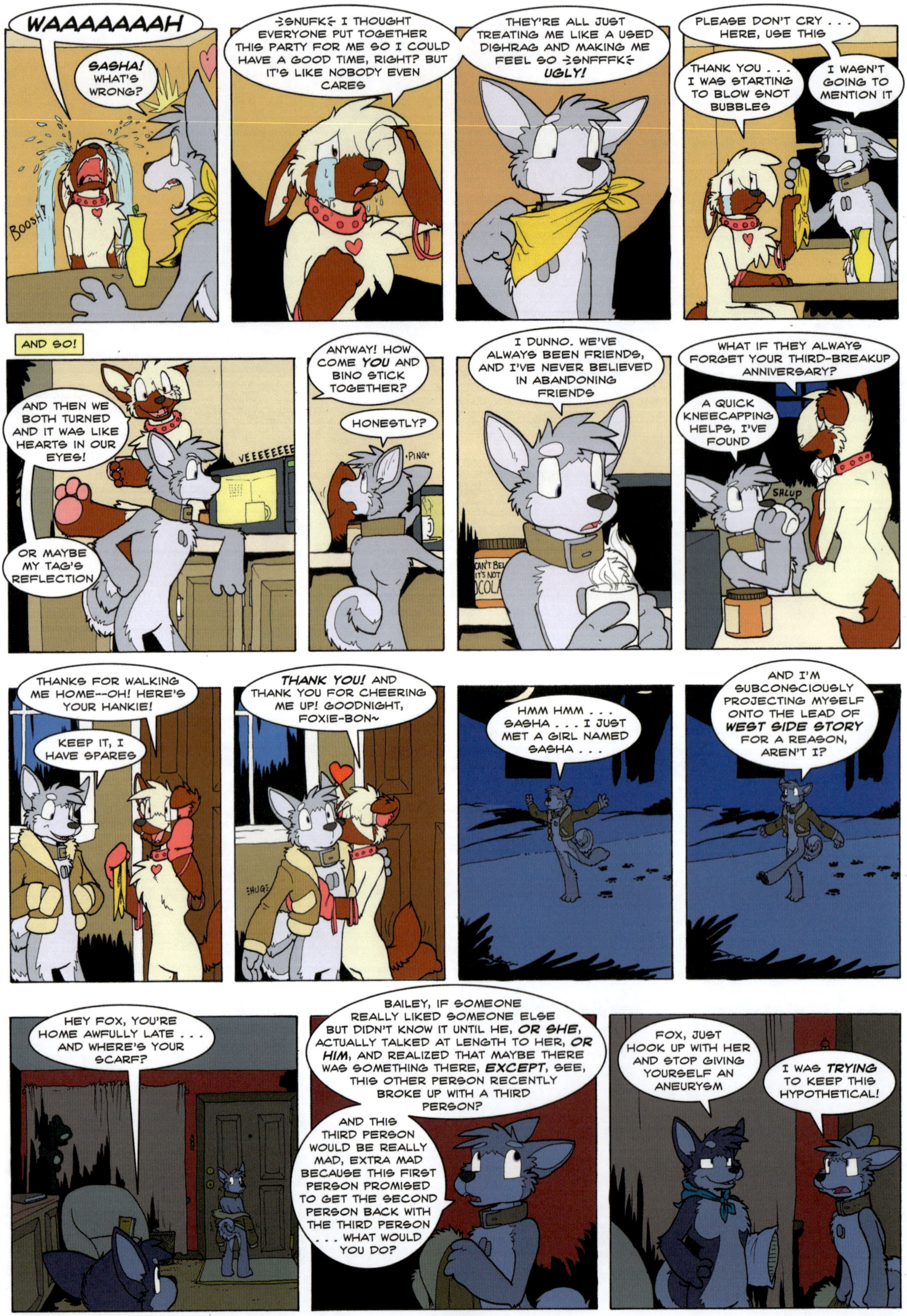
WAAAAAAAH
SASHA! WHAT'S WRONG?
BOOSH!
⊰SNUFK⊱ I THOUGHT EVERYONE PUT TOGETHER THIS PARTY FOR ME SO I COULD HAVE A GOOD TIME, RIGHT? BUT IT'S LIKE NOBODY EVEN CARES
THEY'RE ALL JUST TREATING ME LIKE A USED DISHRAG AND MAKING ME FEEL SO ⊰SNFFFK⊱ UGLY!
PLEASE DON'T CRY . . . HERE, USE THIS
THANK YOU . . . I WAS STARTING TO BLOW SNOT BUBBLES
I WASN'T GOING TO MENTION IT
AND SO!
AND THEN WE BOTH TURNED AND IT WAS LIKE HEARTS IN OUR EYES!
VEEEEEEEE
OR MAYBE MY TAG'S REFLECTION
ANYWAY! HOW COME YOU AND BINO STICK TOGETHER?
HONESTLY?
PING
I DUNNO. WE'VE ALWAYS BEEN FRIENDS, AND I'VE NEVER BELIEVED IN ABANDONING FRIENDS
WHAT IF THEY ALWAYS FORGET YOUR THIRD-BREAKUP ANNIVERSARY?
A QUICK KNEECAPPING HELPS, I'VE FOUND
SHLUP
THANKS FOR WALKING ME HOME--OH! HERE'S YOUR HANKIE!
KEEP IT, I HAVE SPARES
THANK YOU! AND THANK YOU FOR CHEERING ME UP! GOODNIGHT, FOXIE-BON~
HUG
HMM HMM . . . SASHA . . . I JUST MET A GIRL NAMED SASHA . . .
AND I'M SUBCONSCIOUSLY PROJECTING MYSELF ONTO THE LEAD OF WEST SIDE STORY FOR A REASON, AREN'T I?
HEY FOX, YOU'RE HOME AWFULLY LATE . . . AND WHERE'S YOUR SCARF?
BAILEY, IF SOMEONE REALLY LIKED SOMEONE ELSE BUT DIDN'T KNOW IT UNTIL HE, OR SHE, ACTUALLY TALKED AT LENGTH TO HER, OR HIM, AND REALIZED THAT MAYBE THERE WAS SOMETHING THERE, EXCEPT, SEE, THIS OTHER PERSON RECENTLY BROKE UP WITH A THIRD PERSON?
AND THIS THIRD PERSON WOULD BE REALLY MAD, EXTRA MAD BECAUSE THIS FIRST PERSON PROMISED TO GET THE SECOND PERSON BACK WITH THE THIRD PERSON . . . WHAT WOULD YOU DO?
FOX, JUST HOOK UP WITH HER AND STOP GIVING YOURSELF AN ANEURYSM
I WAS TRYING TO KEEP THIS HYPOTHETICAL!

HOW COULD I CALL MYSELF A GOOD BOY IF I TRADE ONE FRIEND SO CALLOUSLY FOR ANOTHER? WHO AM I TO MAKE SUCH JUDGEMENTS?
FOXIE-BON, IT'S GOING TO BE A COLD NIGHT . . . COULD YOU STAY A LITTLE LONGER?
I KNOW IT'S TECHNICALLY MY TURN, BUT SINCE I HAVE A DATE TONIGHT . . .
WHAT THE HOWL HAVE I BEEN DOING ALL THIS TIME?!
SASHA, I HAVE SOMETHING I NEED TO TELL YOU
SO DO I!
TELL YOU I MEAN, NOT . . . YOU KNOW!
THIS IS MY NEW BOYFRIEND KEVIN!
'SUP, TWINKIE?
WE HAD OUR FIRST DATE AT THE DONUT PLACE!
AFTER LAST NIGHT, I WAS GONNA CANCEL, BUT YOU GAVE ME MY CONFIDENCE BACK! ANYWAY, YOU WERE SAYING?
I'LL . . . TELL YOU LATER. YOU GO HAVE FUN
OKAY!
YOU KNOW IF YOU WANTED TO WORK OUT, I COULD GET YOU A PASS FOR THE POLICE GYM
HOW THOUGHTFUL!
SO, ONE OF US WILL NEED TO TELL BINO ABO--
NOT IT
YOU GUYS SUCK!
BINO . . . ABOUT SASHA . . .
OH, ARE YOU STILL ON ABOUT THAT?
BINO!
ARE THESE YOUR PAPERS, PENCIL-NECK?
OH YEAH, "PAPERS", RIGHT HERE
GOOD. AND TAKE OFF THAT TIE, YOU LOOK LIKE A DORK
ANYTHING FOR YOU, DUCHIEPOO!
DON'T CALL ME THAT IN PUBLIC
END

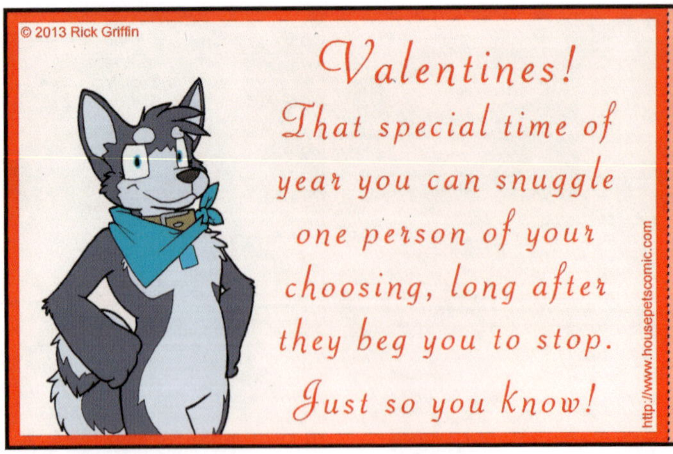
© 2013 Rick Griffin
Valentines!
That special time of year you can snuggle one person of your choosing, long after they beg you to stop.
Just so you know!
http://www.housepetscomic.com

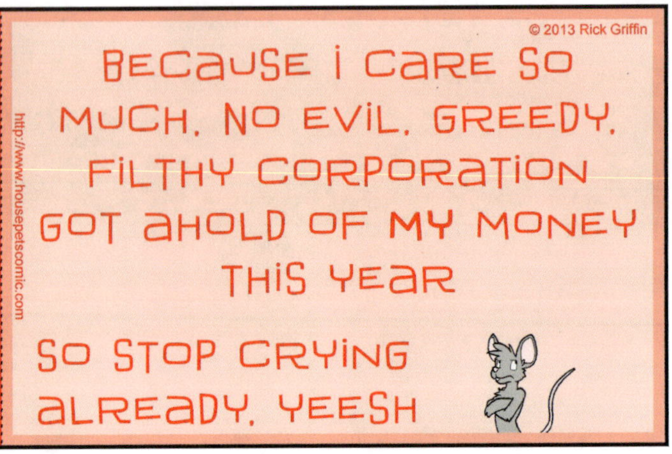
© 2013 Rick Griffin
http://www.housepetscomic.com
BECAUSE I CARE SO MUCH, NO EVIL, GREEDY, FILTHY CORPORATION GOT AHOLD OF MY MONEY THIS YEAR
SO STOP CRYING ALREADY, YEESH

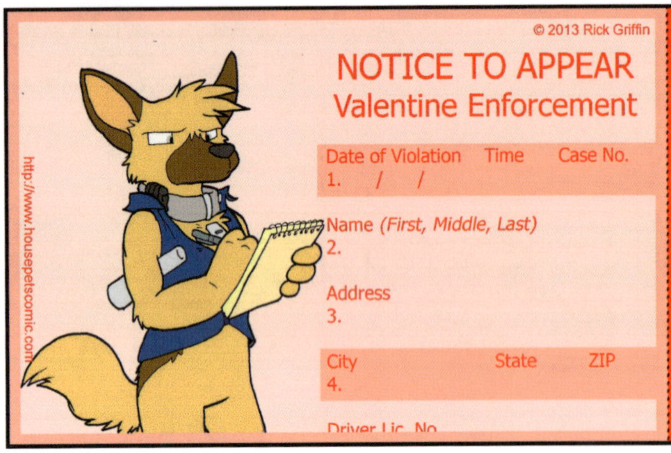
© 2013 Rick Griffin
http://www.housepetscomic.com
NOTICE TO APPEAR
Valentine Enforcement
Date of Violation Time Case No.
1. / /
Name (First, Middle, Last)
2.
Address
3.
City State ZIP
4.

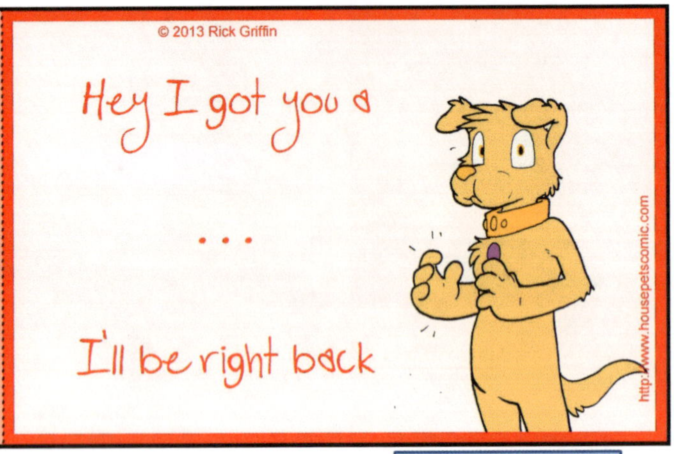
© 2013 Rick Griffin
Hey I got you a
...
I'll be right back
http://www.housepetscomic.com

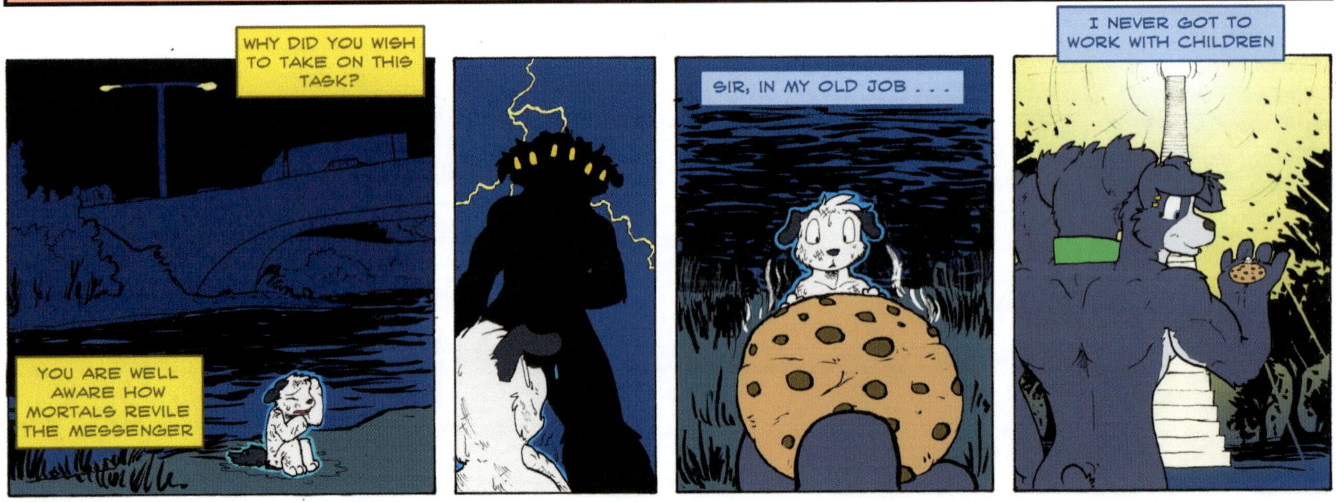
WHY DID YOU WISH TO TAKE ON THIS TASK?
YOU ARE WELL AWARE HOW MORTALS REVILE THE MESSENGER
SIR, IN MY OLD JOB . . .
I NEVER GOT TO WORK WITH CHILDREN

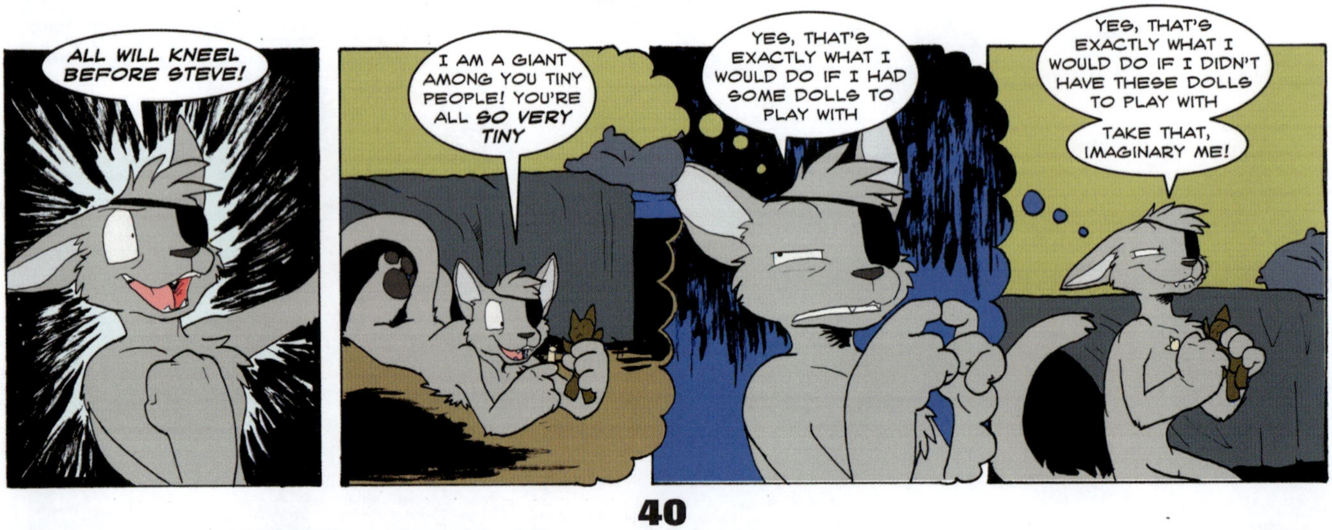
ALL WILL KNEEL BEFORE STEVE!
I AM A GIANT AMONG YOU TINY PEOPLE! YOU'RE ALL SO VERY TINY
YES, THAT'S EXACTLY WHAT I WOULD DO IF I HAD SOME DOLLS TO PLAY WITH
YES, THAT'S EXACTLY WHAT I WOULD DO IF I DIDN'T HAVE THESE DOLLS TO PLAY WITH
TAKE THAT, IMAGINARY ME!

JASPER! WHAT HAVE I TOLD YOU ABOUT SWINGING A HATCHET WILDLY AROUND LOAD-BEARING BEAMS?
LOOK AT ME--ONE OF THESE DAYS YOU WON'T FLATTEN INTO AN AMUSING ACCORDIAN SHAPE. IS ONE BROWN MOUSE REALLY WORTH THAT?
SPEAK OF THE DEVIL . . . HOW IS HE CARRYING THAT PAIR OF GARDEN SHEARS? AND IS THAT A DUCKLING WITH HIM?
OH, YOU'RE GONNA CHASE HIM ANYWAY, OKAY. WATCH OUT FOR THE--
VRRRCH
--YEAH, YOU'RE GONNA GET THAT
SEVEN HUNDRED?! ELAINE'LL KILL ME!
I TOLD YOU NOT TO USE OUR YARD AS YOUR PERSONAL STORAGE!
BUT A FINE?! CAN'T THE MILTONS' FANCY LAWYER CLEAR THIS FOR US?
Housepets!
Jack Of One Trade
THAT LAWYER IS NOT A GET-OUT-OF-JAIL-FREE CARD! WE'RE STILL RESPONSIBLE, AND BY EXTENSION, YOU ARE RESPONSIBLE
. . . YOU MADE YOUR MARK ON IT AFTER ALL
STOP HOLDING IT LIKE A DEN MOTHER!
I'M FINE IF YOU USE THE GARAGE FOR YOUR STOREFRONT, BUT ISN'T THIS SIDESTEPPING THE PROBLEM?
WHAT DO YOU MEAN?
ISN'T MOST OF THIS STUFF STOLEN, "FOUR FINGER DISCOUNT"?
MILES, I'M SHOCKED! YOU KNOW I'VE BEEN CLEAN FOR YEARS!
THAT . . . THAT'S A REFLEX

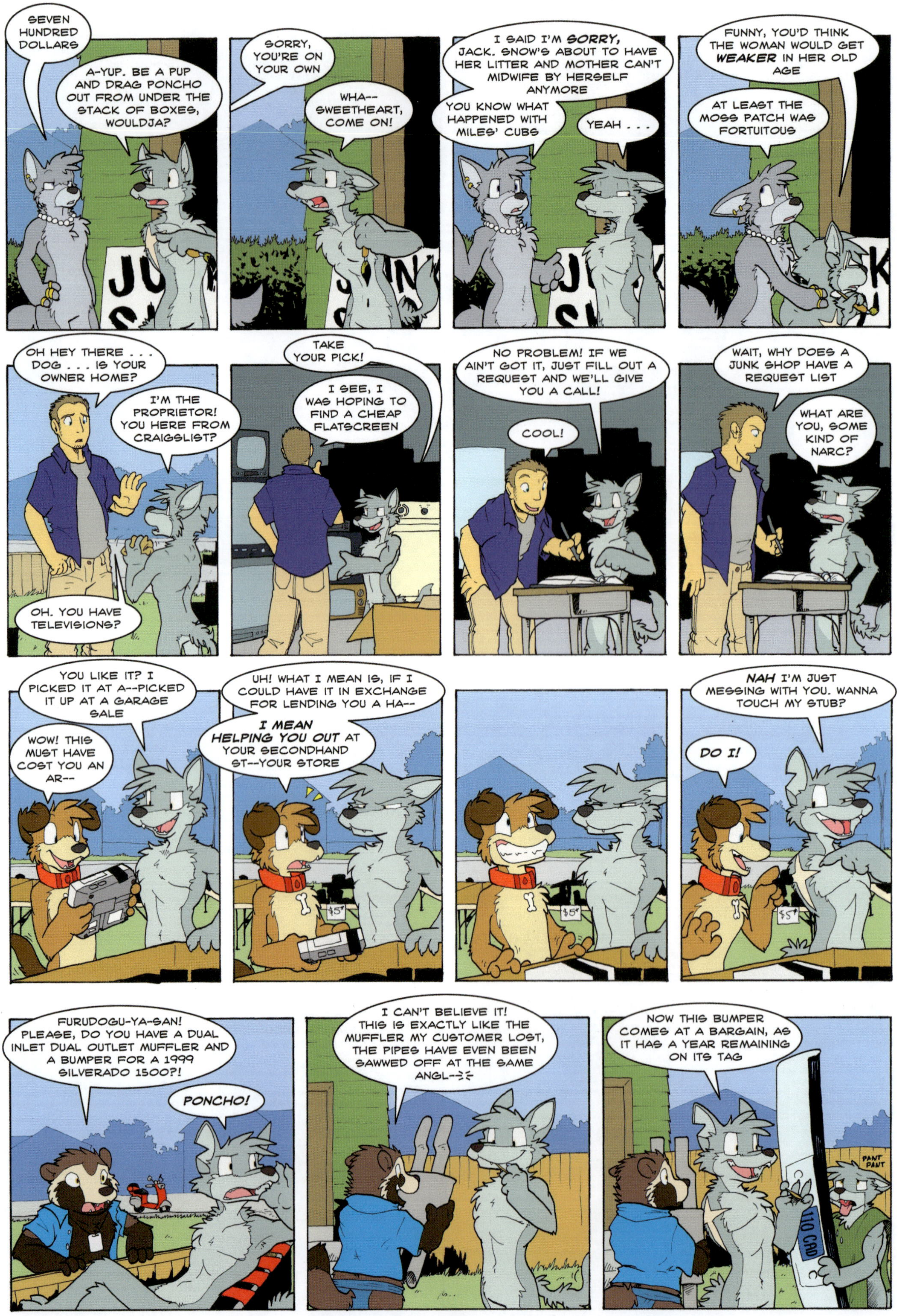
SEVEN HUNDRED DOLLARS
A-YUP. BE A PUP AND DRAG PONCHO OUT FROM UNDER THE STACK OF BOXES, WOULDJA?
SORRY, YOU'RE ON YOUR OWN
WHA-- SWEETHEART, COME ON!
I SAID I'M SORRY, JACK. SNOW'S ABOUT TO HAVE HER LITTER AND MOTHER CAN'T MIDWIFE BY HERSELF ANYMORE
YOU KNOW WHAT HAPPENED WITH MILES' CUBS
YEAH . . .
FUNNY, YOU'D THINK THE WOMAN WOULD GET WEAKER IN HER OLD AGE
AT LEAST THE MOSS PATCH WAS FORTUITOUS
OH HEY THERE . . . DOG . . . IS YOUR OWNER HOME?
I'M THE PROPRIETOR! YOU HERE FROM CRAIGSLIST?
OH. YOU HAVE TELEVISIONS?
TAKE YOUR PICK!
I SEE, I WAS HOPING TO FIND A CHEAP FLATSCREEN
NO PROBLEM! IF WE AIN'T GOT IT, JUST FILL OUT A REQUEST AND WE'LL GIVE YOU A CALL!
COOL!
WAIT, WHY DOES A JUNK SHOP HAVE A REQUEST LIST
WHAT ARE YOU, SOME KIND OF NARC?
YOU LIKE IT? I PICKED IT AT A--PICKED IT UP AT A GARAGE SALE
WOW! THIS MUST HAVE COST YOU AN AR--
UH! WHAT I MEAN IS, IF I COULD HAVE IT IN EXCHANGE FOR LENDING YOU A HA--
I MEAN HELPING YOU OUT AT YOUR SECONDHAND ST--YOUR STORE
$5
NAH I'M JUST MESSING WITH YOU. WANNA TOUCH MY STUB?
DO I!
FURUDOGU-YA-SAN! PLEASE, DO YOU HAVE A DUAL INLET DUAL OUTLET MUFFLER AND A BUMPER FOR A 1999 SILVERADO 1500?!
PONCHO!
I CAN'T BELIEVE IT! THIS IS EXACTLY LIKE THE MUFFLER MY CUSTOMER LOST, THE PIPES HAVE EVEN BEEN SAWWED OFF AT THE SAME ANGL--
NOW THIS BUMPER COMES AT A BARGAIN, AS IT HAS A YEAR REMAINING ON ITS TAG
PANT PANT
110 CAD

EXCUSE ME, WE RECEIVED INFORMATION ABOUT A ONE-ARMED BANDIT--
!
CLOSED
WHAM
LOOKS LIKE WE'LL HAVE TO COME BACK LATER
AWW
JACKPOT
K-9
LUCRETIA TOOK PITY ON US AND MADE SOME LEMONADE. LEAST THAT'S WHAT IT SMELLS LIKE
THANKS
I'M GOING UP IN THE MORNING WITH MR. LONDON TO PAY THE FINE. STILL THINK IT AIN'T NOTHING BUT A LOAD
I KNOW WHAT YOU MEAN! HUMANS ARE ALL ABOUT THINGS, BUT THEY PENALIZE US FOR HAVING THINGS!?
IF THERE'S ANYTHING YOU CAN COUNT ON US WOLVES FOR, IT'S TOTAL FAIRNESS!
HEAR HEAR!
HERE'S YOUR MONEY. AND MY CON-SEE-URGE MR. LONDON IS HERE WITH ME TO MAKE SURE I AIN'T SWINDLED, ON ACCOUNT OF BEING CANINE-AMERICAN
THAT IS REASONABLE, MR. THE WOLF
ERM, THERE APPEARS TO BE SEVEN THOUSAND DOLLARS HERE, BUT THE BILL IS ONLY FOR SEVEN HUNDRED
WELL LAH-DEE-DAH, LOOK AT THE BIG CITY CLERK WITH HIS BIG CITY "EDUCATION!
THAT WAS ACTUALLY DIRECTED AT YOUR LAWYER
LOOK, MATH IS HARD!
END

WHY DIDN'T YOU COME TO ME? I THINK IT'S A GREAT IDEA!
I'M SORRY, BUT I DON'T THINK WE NEED HELP IN GETTING MARRIED
Housepets!
The King And I
MILTON MANOR
HOME OF THE MILTON FERRETS (THE LEGAL OWNERS OF THE WOLVES, ALSO KING)
NATURALLY. I DON'T WANT TO TELL YOU YOUR BUSINESS! I'LL JUST WORK AROUND THE DETAILS OF YOUR EXTENSIVE PLANS
ORANG
SO! TELL ME WHAT YOU'VE ACCOMPLISHED BETWEEN CHRISTMAS AND NOW
I FOUND OUT WHAT A WEDDING DRESS IS
HOW MARVELOUS
. . . SHE'S STILL MY DOG, RIGHT?
OH, SURE, SURE!
SHE MIGHT OCCASIONALLY STAY AT THE WOLF HOUSE, OR KING WITH YOU, BUT ALL I'M ASKING IS YOU DON'T SEPARATE THEM
HUH
SO WHO GETS THE PUPPIES?
DADDY!
I THINK YOU'RE MISSING THE POINT HERE MR. LINDBERG
SO KEENE'S HELPING US FOR SOME KIND OF "PLAN" TO MAKE ANIMALS AND HUMANS EQUAL, AND NOT OUT OF THE GOODNESS OF HIS HEART?
I HAVE NO IDEA WHERE HE FALLS ON THE GOOD/EVIL SCALE SO I CAN'T SAY
I DON'T WANT OUR LOVE TO BE EXPLOITED FOR SOMEONE'S SCHEME
HON, THIS IS HARDLY EXPLOITATIVE
ANIMAL PLANET SIX-PART MINISERIES, HERE WE COME!
NOW IT'S EXPLOITATIVE
YOU'RE GIVING US A HONEYMOON TOO?!
SURE! I HAVE A DOZEN HOUSES GOING UNUSED AT ANY GIVEN TIME
THAT'S GENEROUS OF YOU!
PROVIDED OF COURSE THAT ROCK'S CAMERA CREW BE THERE TO DOCU--

SO, ARE YOU TWO . . . COMPATIBLE?
I GUESS?
REV. GURNEY MARRIAGE COUNSELOR
SORRY, IT'S . . . I'VE NEVER DONE THIS WITH DOGS BEFORE
WHY SHOULD THAT MATTER? JUST TREAT US LIKE WE'RE PEOPLE
THEN I SUPPOSE I WOULD ASK, WHAT MAKES YOU THINK YOU'RE RIGHT FOR EACH OTHER?
WHEN I SEE SMALLER DOGS ACROSS THE STREET I USUALLY BARK AT THEM, BUT I DON'T BARK AT KING!
I SEE
OH BOY, CHORES. MY FAVORITE THING IN THE WHOLE WORLD
I KNOW, RIGHT?!
WAIT, "REGISTER"? DIDN'T WE ALREADY DO THAT?
OH, NO, THIS IS GIFT REGISTRY; YOU PICK A STORE AND COMPILE A LIST OF THINGS YOU WANT AS WEDDING PRESENTS
PET ZONE
LARGE TRAVEL CAGE
SURPRISINGLY, WE APPEAR TO BE EQUIPPED FOR THIS
ORMATION
OH GOOD, WE DIDN'T WANT THIS TO BE WEIRD OR ANYTHING
THE DRESS WILL BE MODIFIED, OF COURSE, BUT KEEPING THE DESIGN INTACT FOR YOUR SIZE, WE MAY BE BETTER OFF ALTERING A FLOWER GIRL OUTFIT. AS FOR THE SHEDDING . . .
KING KNOWS A LOT ABOUT CLOTHES . . . WHY DIDN'T HE TELL ME THIS WOULD BE SO COMPLICATED?
HAL'S COSTUMES
NAH, JUST SHOVE IT IN A PAPER BAG
SECRET AGENT AGE 5-7
OH, I GET! YOU WANT I SHOULD MAKE A DOGGIE CAKE! I HAVE A DESIGN SHAPE LIKE SNOOPY DOGHOUSE!
NO! NO SILLY THEMES!
THIS IS A SERIOUS CEREMONY AND WE WANT AN ELEGANT MODERN DESIGN!
AND IT CAN'T HAVE ANY CHOCOLATE. AND THE TOPPER NEEDS TO BE OF DOGS
ALSO HALF OF IT NEEDS TO BE MADE OF HAMBURGER
MAYBE A LITTLE THEMING IS IN ORDER

Panel 1: IT LOOKS LIKE WE'RE ALMOST DONE! / WAIT, AREN'T WE MISSING SOMETHING? SHOULDN'T WE BE LOOKING FOR A PHOTOGRAPHER?

Panel 2: (no dialogue)

Panel 3: RIGHT, I'M AN IDIOT / GUYS, FOR THE LAST TIME...

Panel 4: SMALLER BENCHES UP FRONT, MOVE SOME PEWS OUT IF YOU HAVE TO! / THIS IS BOTH SMALLER THAN I THOUGHT YOU'D PICK AND LARGER THAN WE NEED

Panel 5: WHY? EVEN TREATING THIS AS A SEMI-PRIVATE WEDDING THE GUEST LIST IS FAIRLY BIG / BUT WHO ALL IS COMING FOR BAILEY'S SIDE? SHE'S NEW AROUND HERE / DON'T FORGET MR. LINDBERG OWNS HER / RIGHT, THE POLICE OFF--

Panel 6: ...WE'RE GOING TO HAVE FERAL WOLVES DIRECTLY ACROSS THE AISLE FROM POLICE DOGS?! / LOOK, WORST COMES TO WORST, THE AMERICA'S FUNNIEST VIDEOS WINNINGS SHOULD COVER THE DEPOSIT

Panel 7: IT WASN'T NECESSARY TO DRESS UP FOR REHEARSAL, BUT AT LEAST WE KNOW WE NEED THE AC ON "DARK SIDE OF THE MOON" / THANKS, I'LL GO PASS OUT ON THE BENCH NOW

Panel 8: NO SASHA, BEING THE BRIDESMAID DOESN'T MEAN YOU HAVE TO MARRY THE GROOMSMAN / WELL GOOD, MY BOYFRIEND IS GONNA BE HERE AND THAT'D BE TOTALLY AWKWARD!

Panel 9: IS IT BAD IF THE FLOWER GIRL SWALLOWS THE RING? / THIS IS WHY THE PRACTICE RING WAS MADE OF PRETZEL

Panel 10: AND I SAY I DO, THAT'S THE EASY PART / THEN THE POWER VESTED IN ME, YADDA YADDA, YOU'RE MARRIED

Panel 11: YAY YOU'RE MARRIED! I'M SO HAPPY FOR YOU! / ACK--SASHA! THIS IS JUST A REHEARSAL! / GLOMP

Panel 12: THEN ARE YOU SAYING THAT YOU WERE INSINCERE?! / I'M SAYING WE NEED TO VERY CALMLY REVIEW SOME BASIC PRINCIPLES

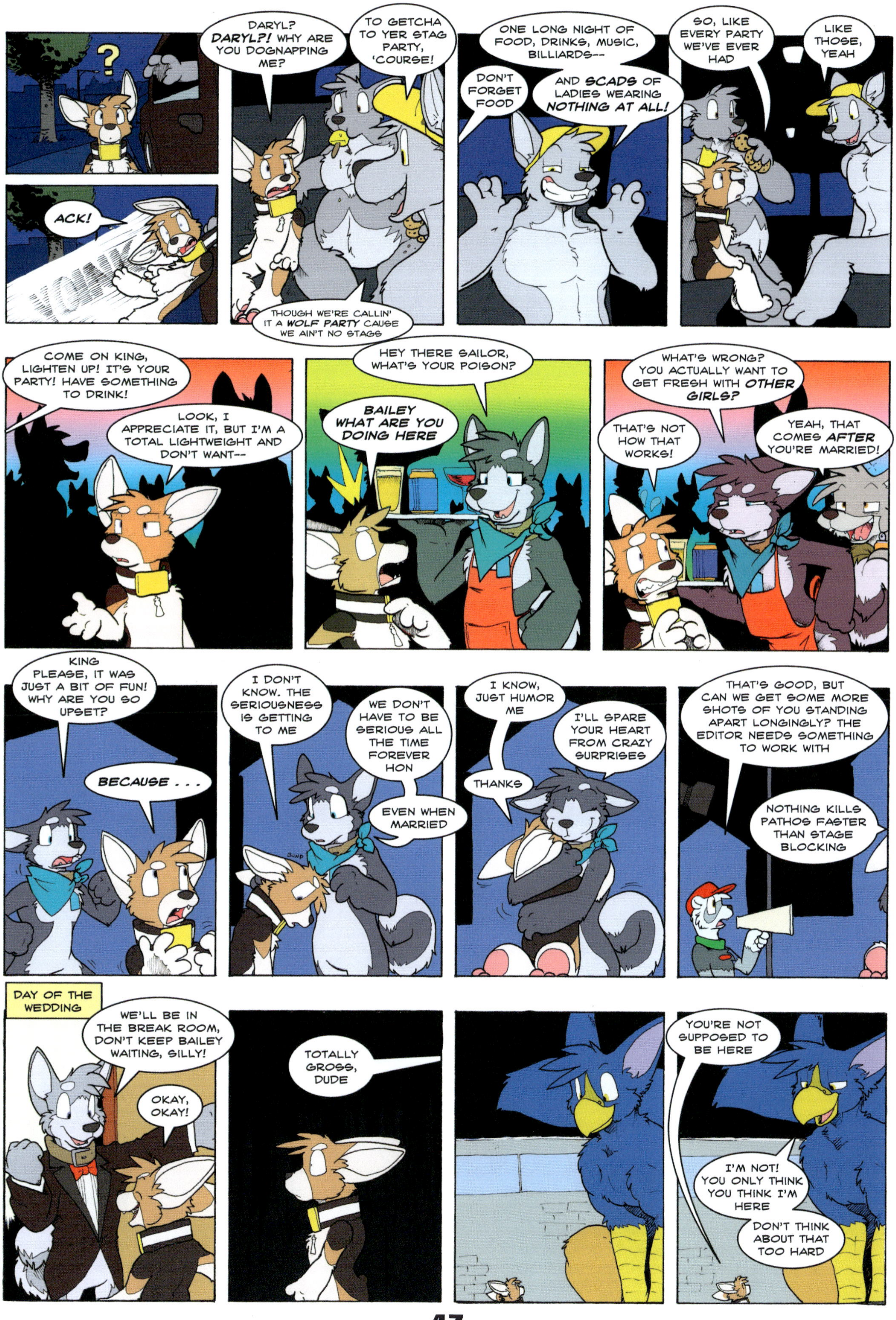
?
ACK!
YOINK
DARYL? DARYL?! WHY ARE YOU DOGNAPPING ME?
TO GETCHA TO YER STAG PARTY, 'COURSE!
THOUGH WE'RE CALLIN' IT A WOLF PARTY CAUSE WE AIN'T NO STAGS
ONE LONG NIGHT OF FOOD, DRINKS, MUSIC, BILLIARDS--
DON'T FORGET FOOD
AND SCADS OF LADIES WEARING NOTHING AT ALL!
SO, LIKE EVERY PARTY WE'VE EVER HAD
LIKE THOSE, YEAH
COME ON KING, LIGHTEN UP! IT'S YOUR PARTY! HAVE SOMETHING TO DRINK!
LOOK, I APPRECIATE IT, BUT I'M A TOTAL LIGHTWEIGHT AND DON'T WANT--
HEY THERE SAILOR, WHAT'S YOUR POISON?
BAILEY WHAT ARE YOU DOING HERE
WHAT'S WRONG? YOU ACTUALLY WANT TO GET FRESH WITH OTHER GIRLS?
THAT'S NOT HOW THAT WORKS!
YEAH, THAT COMES AFTER YOU'RE MARRIED!
KING PLEASE, IT WAS JUST A BIT OF FUN! WHY ARE YOU SO UPSET?
BECAUSE . . .
I DON'T KNOW. THE SERIOUSNESS IS GETTING TO ME
WE DON'T HAVE TO BE SERIOUS ALL THE TIME FOREVER HON
EVEN WHEN MARRIED
I KNOW, JUST HUMOR ME
I'LL SPARE YOUR HEART FROM CRAZY SURPRISES
THANKS
THAT'S GOOD, BUT CAN WE GET SOME MORE SHOTS OF YOU STANDING APART LONGINGLY? THE EDITOR NEEDS SOMETHING TO WORK WITH
NOTHING KILLS PATHOS FASTER THAN STAGE BLOCKING
DAY OF THE WEDDING
WE'LL BE IN THE BREAK ROOM, DON'T KEEP BAILEY WAITING, SILLY!
OKAY, OKAY!
TOTALLY GROSS, DUDE
YOU'RE NOT SUPPOSED TO BE HERE
I'M NOT! YOU ONLY THINK YOU THINK I'M HERE
DON'T THINK ABOUT THAT TOO HARD

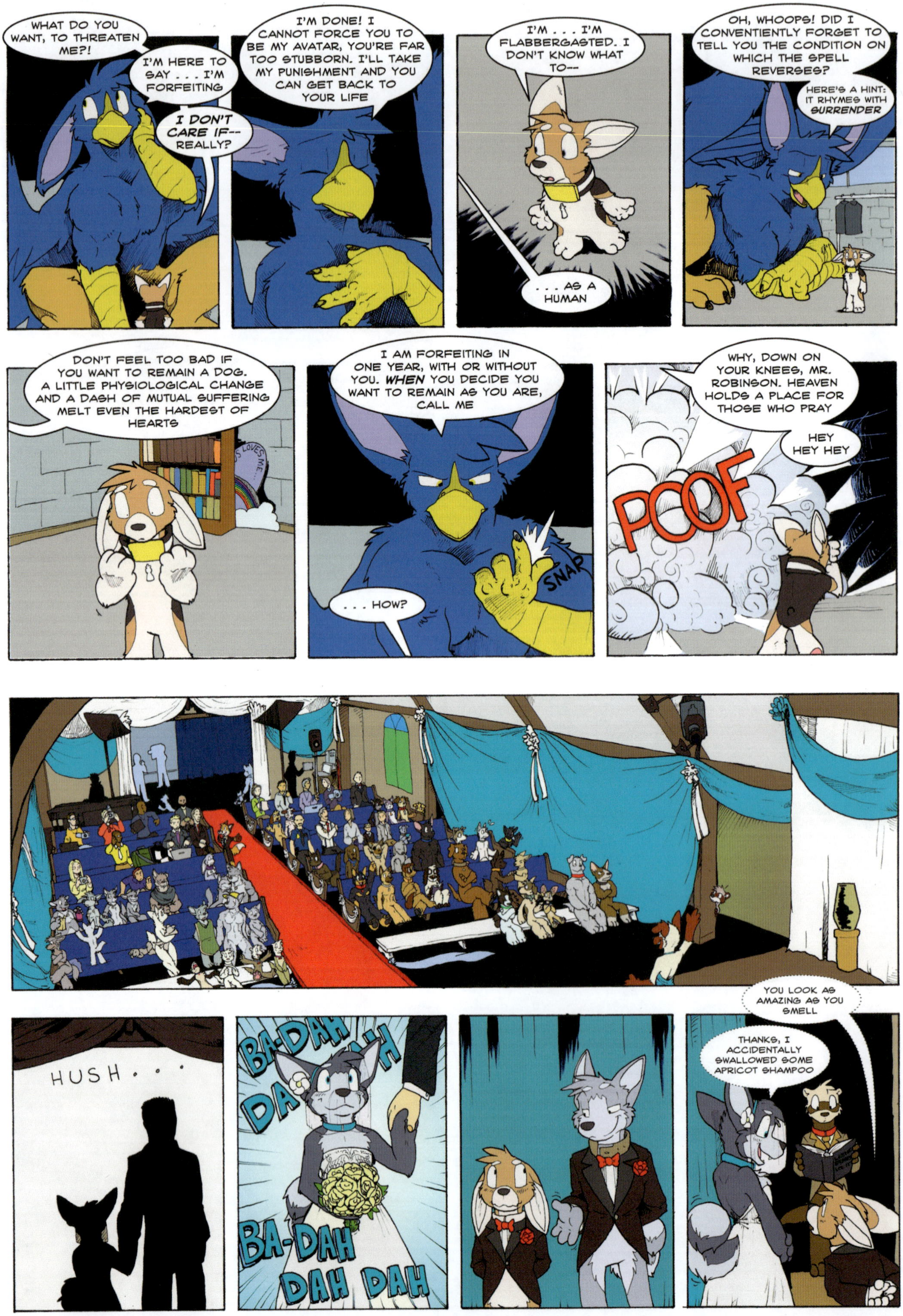
WHAT DO YOU WANT, TO THREATEN ME?!
I'M HERE TO SAY . . . I'M FORFEITING
I DON'T CARE IF-- REALLY?
I'M DONE! I CANNOT FORCE YOU TO BE MY AVATAR, YOU'RE FAR TOO STUBBORN. I'LL TAKE MY PUNISHMENT AND YOU CAN GET BACK TO YOUR LIFE
I'M . . . I'M FLABBERGASTED. I DON'T KNOW WHAT TO--
. . . AS A HUMAN
OH, WHOOPS! DID I CONVENTIENTLY FORGET TO TELL YOU THE CONDITION ON WHICH THE SPELL REVERSES?
HERE'S A HINT: IT RHYMES WITH SURRENDER
DON'T FEEL TOO BAD IF YOU WANT TO REMAIN A DOG. A LITTLE PHYSIOLOGICAL CHANGE AND A DASH OF MUTUAL SUFFERING MELT EVEN THE HARDEST OF HEARTS
I AM FORFEITING IN ONE YEAR, WITH OR WITHOUT YOU. WHEN YOU DECIDE YOU WANT TO REMAIN AS YOU ARE, CALL ME
SNAP
. . . HOW?
WHY, DOWN ON YOUR KNEES, MR. ROBINSON. HEAVEN HOLDS A PLACE FOR THOSE WHO PRAY
HEY HEY HEY
POOF
HUSH . . .
BA-DAH DAH DAH
BA-DAH DAH DAH
YOU LOOK AS AMAZING AS YOU SMELL
THANKS, I ACCIDENTALLY SWALLOWED SOME APRICOT SHAMPOO

Panel 1: ...DEARLY BELOVED, WE ARE GATHERED HERE TO GET THROUGH THIS THING CALLED LIFE. WE ARE HERE TO HONOR THESE TWO...

Panel 2: ...THAT THEY MAY BE JOINED IN (HOLY) MATRIMONY, REACHING THIS DECISION EITHER OF THEIR OWN FREE WILL OR BY SEVERE BRAIN DAMAGE, EITHER BY INTENT OR ACT OF GOD...

Panel 3: LADIES AND GENTLEMEN AND DOGS, IF ANYONE HAS REASON WHY THESE TWO SHOULD NOT BE WED...

Panel 4: ...TELL IT TO MY SECRET GOON SQUAD

Panel 5: BY THE "POWER" VESTED IN ME BY THE STATE OF ≋COUGH! COUGH COUGH!≋ I NOW PRONOUNCE YOU DOG AND WIFE

YOU MAY KISS THE BRIDE

Panel 6: WHATEVER THE COST MAY BE...

CLAP CLAP CLAP WOOOO! GO KING! CLAP CLAP CLAP AROOO! *WHISTLE!*

...I WILL MOVE HEAVEN AND EARTH TO GET TO YOU

Panel 7: ARE YOU MARRIED *NOW*?

I DON'T KNOW, LET ME GET A FEW MORE SMOOCHES IN TO MAKE SURE IT TOOK

49

Panel 1: "WHY DOES EVERYONE SEEM TO GO BONKERS OVER STUPID HUMAN THINGS?"

"YEAH I KNOW, RIGHT? THEY LOOK SO DUMB"

Panel 3: "MAYBE *WE* COULD GET MARRIED SOMETIME"

END!

50

MR. BIGGLESWORTH

SQUEAK
BRUCE
ROOSEVELT

SPO

DUCHESS

51

Next time, on
Housepets!

"OOH, YOU HAVE REALLY STRONG TOES... PRESS A LITTLE DEEPER, HON, I CAN TAKE IT~"

SQUEEEEEEE
"AA AAAAA AAH!"

"LIVE FAST! DIE YOUNG! LEAVE A PICKLED CORPSE!"

"O PETE WHO ART IN HEAVEN... I HAVE A GREAT BURDEN ON MY MIND, AND I CANNOT BEAR IT ANY LONGER..."